# THE REAPER OF ZION

## A HARRY BAUER THRILLER

## BLAKE BANNER

RIGHTHOUSE

# PRAISE FOR HARRY BAUER

ISBN-13: 978-1-63696-451-5

ISBN-10: 1-63696-451-6

Printed in the United States of America

www.righthouse.com

www.instagram.com/righthousebooks

www.facebook.com/righthousebooks

twitter.com/righthousebooks

## HARRY BAUER THRILLER SERIES

# ONE

It was August in New York. It didn't seem so inviting. It was five p.m., and we were only in the mid eighties, but it wasn't the heat. It was the humidity. I was in my study with my back turned to my desk and my feet on the windowsill, looking down on the brownstones of James Baldwin Place. It was a nice view, but it didn't help much.

Behind me, as I said, was my desk. On it was an old, blue Olivetti portable typewriter. Because I had read in the Free Press about a journalist who had sold his laptop and his cell phone and wrote everything on a typewriter, the way they used to when we were men and wore hats and women had a sense of humor. He said he was a happier man for doing that.

Beside the typewriter was a single page that said, in capitals, SOLDIER OF FORTUNE – MEMOIRS OF A PROFESSIONAL HIT MAN. Bottom right was my address, and bottom left was my claim to copyright.

Rolled into the typewriter was a second sheet of paper with the word *One* centered at the top, and two spaces below that,

*The most interesting parts about what I am about to tell you are the parts I cannot tell you.*

Having written that self-defeating line, I had picked up my glass of whiskey, spun my chair, put my feet on the windowsill, and started staring at the brownstones, half secluded by trees, on James Baldwin Place.

That was when I saw the woman. Hammett and Spillane would have called her a dame, and she was all that. I figured she was five-five with generous curves but a slim waist. Her legs were long and shapely in jeans that were hugging her like they never wanted to let go. Mother Nature was all present and correct under her black T-shirt, and her face, from what I could see through my third-floor window, was cute and sweet, framed by the blackest hair I had ever seen. Chandler had said of a woman once that she would make a bishop kick a hole in a stained glass window. This was that dame.

She was walking slowly, looking at the doors like she was searching for an address. When she drew level with my house, she crossed over. I had time to frown into my whiskey before the doorbell chimed. I didn't turn, but I listened and heard Rosalia, my new housekeeper, cross the entrance hall and open the door. I listened some more, this time to the silence that followed, and then to the feet that thumped up the stairs. My study door opened, and I swung around to see Rosalia leaning against the jamb and perspiring.

"There is lady wanna see you, Mr. Bauer. She say is very important. She look nice."

I smiled with little feeling and said, "Send her up."

I drained my glass and stood as I heard the lighter steps ascending. They paused, and I saw the woman I had been watching a moment earlier lean across the doorway to peer in. Close up, I figured she was in her mid to late thirties. She smiled, and it was like somebody had turned the lights on. I couldn't help smiling back.

I crossed the room toward her and said, "If you lean too far, you might fall over. Come on in. How can I help you?"

She straightened up and crossed the threshold. "You're Harry Bauer?"

"In the Army they called me Bauer, Harry, when they weren't calling me other things. But yeah, I am Harry Bauer."

I gestured her toward a comfortable green chesterfield on the near side of my desk.

"Please sit down. I am curious..." I trailed off, not sure how to finish the sentence.

"Samuel Cotton gave me your name," she said. "He said you'd be able to help me."

My eyebrows rose of their own accord. "Sam?" I said. "You're friends?"

"No, not really. It's complicated." She started to smile but seemed to think better of it. "Somebody suggested I speak to him, and he recommended you. I hope you are not going to recommend somebody else."

"I hope not too," I said with more feeling than I intended. "But you'll have to tell me what you want help with. Why not start by telling me who *you* are?"

She was still standing, looking uncertain. She moved to the green chesterfield at the desk and sat. I returned to my own seat. She spent a couple of moments looking at her thumbs in her lap, then said, "My name is Miriam Benzaquen. I am from Israel. I lost my husband and my two children on October 7th, almost two years ago. My husband and my son were killed, mercifully, and my daughter was abducted."

I felt my skin go cold. Inside, the emptiness of hopelessness seemed to open up, like it was trying to draw me in. I heard myself say, "I am so sorry," but the words were as empty and hopeless as the void inside me.

"The deaths of my son and my husband are..." She trailed off, lifted her eyes, and looked at me for the first time since she'd started talking. "That is damage that will not be mended until I join them in heaven. But my daughter—" She held my eye for a long moment. "She has to come home."

I nodded. There was an inevitableness to what she said. I had no choice but to agree. I said, "Yes."

"But"—she took a deep breath—"there is something else."

"What?"

"Yahya Sinwar—you know who he was?"

"Of course. He was the head of Hamas."

"He was the mastermind behind the attack on October 7th, and he was reported killed by the IDF. But there was another who assisted him, who was one of the leaders of the attack. His name is Mohammed Abbasid. He perpetrated horrors on his living victims that cannot be imagined. He filmed them, and he filmed his men performing these acts, laughing and boasting. He is still alive."

"I've seen the films."

"I am not a rich woman, Mr. Bauer, but I will pay you whatever you ask for. Just bring back my daughter and punish this man for what he has done."

"What's your daughter's name?"

"Sandra. She turned fifteen last November." Her gaze drifted out the window and spoke as though to herself. "Next November she'll turn sixteen."

For a moment which felt oddly surreal, I stared at the ancient typewriter in front of me, beside it the page: *SOLDIER OF FORTUNE - MEMOIRS OF A PROFESSIONAL HIT MAN*, and rolled into the typewriter, *One, The most interesting parts about what I am about to tell you are the parts I cannot tell you.*

I gave a small sigh. I was going to write my memoirs, but you can't tell a story until that story is finished. My story was not finished.

She started speaking again.

"We lived at the kibbutz at Kfar Aza. They came across the field. There was no time to prepare a defense. The civil guards were volunteers, veterans from the IDF. They made it to the armory, where the rifles were kept, and there they were overwhelmed and killed. Then the..." She trailed off, looking from wall to wall as though searching for some kind of reason or logic. "I can't call them men. They were not men. They were like beings possessed by evil. Three hundred of them moved through the streets." She stared at me and frowned. "There was no system, no method, no logic. Some houses they burned, some houses they went in and massacred the inhabitants. They beheaded children, burned families alive."

She paused, and we sat in silence. Her gaze drifted from my face to the desk. "My husband died at the armory. He took seven shots, and I pray every day that his death was quick and God gathered him to his bosom."

She went suddenly very still and silent.

"David, my son." She stopped and started again. "Some houses they ignored, others they attacked. It seemed random. We saw them come toward our house, toward the door, and my son, David, snatched the big knife from the kitchen and ran out to confront them. He was twelve. His sister and I ran out after him. They laughed and shot him in his legs. Then they decapitated him with his own knife.

"Two of them took my daughter. Another punched me to the ground and was going to rape me, but they called him from a house across the road. He kicked me in my stomach and my head. I don't remember anything else."

We sat in silence for a while. It was like an unspoken gesture of respect for the fallen. Eventually I said, "You don't need to pay me anything, Miriam. I'll do everything I can to bring your daughter back."

She barely acknowledged it. She gave the smallest of nods, as though accepting the inevitable. When she spoke again, it was barely a whisper. "I feel so much hatred, Mr. Bauer. I feel as though they infected me with their darkness, with their evil. I don't want this hatred. I don't want it inside me. But I think of Joseph—my husband was Joseph—and I think of my son, David, and Sandra, screaming as they carried her away. And all I can feel, Mr. Bauer, is black hatred. Hatred so deep I cannot describe it."

There was nothing I could say. I drew breath, hesitating, but before I could say anything, she said, "The man who took my daughter, I have seen videos and photographs of him since. He is Mohammed Abbasid."

I nodded. After a moment, I leaned forward with my elbows on the desk and spoke quietly, looking into her large, dark eyes.

"I will kill Mohammed Abbasid and as many of his men as are still alive. I said a moment ago that you did not need to pay me. I take that back."

Her eyes were dull when she asked, "How much do you want?"

I shook my head. "Not how much. What. I want a promise. The promise comes with two sides, like a coin."

"What promise?"

"On one side I want you to promise me that you will never stop hating these beings for what they did. As humans we have to hate them and everything they stand for, and we have to fight against them as long as we have life in us. On the other hand, I want you to promise me that you will lay that hate to one side and focus your mind, your heart, and your soul on honoring everything your husband and your son died to uphold and help your daughter to find love and joy. I can free her physically, but you and she have to work together to free her mind and her soul from the memories."

She stared at me for a long time, but eventually she nodded. "I promise."

"Is there a number where I can contact you if I need to?"

She reached in her bag and pulled out a violet card with white script on it. It had her address in Tel Aviv and her telephone number. It said she was a florist.

"When do you return to Israel, Mrs. Benzaquen?"

"Miriam. I suppose that, given the enterprise we have entered into together, we should be on first name terms, Harry. Is that all right?"

I managed a smile. "Of course. When do you fly back, Miriam?"

"Tomorrow evening, unless you need me to stay for any reason."

"No, that's fine. Stay safe."

She gave a short laugh and got to her feet. "These days? It is hard to know if you are safer in New York or Tel Aviv. The world seems to be moving again to such a dark place. What is happening, Harry?"

"I don't know. I often wonder."

"The unholy trinity: burn the books, kill free speech, and exterminate the Jews. My rabbi says the Nephilim are awakening."

"I'm a hardnosed atheist, Miriam, and I am not given to

pretty, flowery speeches. But I do know that we must fight, like Churchill said, fight on the beaches and the landing grounds, and never surrender. And we can only do that if we own the hate and never let the hate own us."

She stared into my eyes for a moment, then laid her left hand over my heart and smiled.

"You are a strange man, Harry."

"That's what the midwife told—"

"Don't. I'll look forward to hearing from you. If you need anything, anything at all, let me know."

And then she was gone, and the door closed behind her leaving a strange emptiness in the room and the faint aroma of jasmine.

I returned to the desk and sat looking at the telephone on my desk. I had bought the relic at the same time as the Olivetti. I dialed a secure number, and after a moment, the brigadier's voice said, "Harry."

"Sir, I need to talk to you."

"Is it urgent?"

"Yeah."

"Come over. I'm at my apartment. We'll have a drink and an early dinner."

"Sounds good, sir. I'll be there in an hour."

I hung up and found I was still staring at the phone, only now I was frowning. Why I wasn't sure, but something in my gut was frowning and making my face frown too.

# TWO

We were sitting on his penthouse terrace overlooking Riverside Drive, Riverside Park, and the great, dark wash of the Hudson on its slow, stately path to the North Atlantic. There was an abundance of potted plants and flowers around us, all with a variety of citrus smells that he claimed kept away the wasps and the flies in that sultry weather. He held a tall gin and tonic with lots of ice, and he was frowning at me from behind big, black Wayfarers.

He had fixed me what he called a tall Leggero martini cocktail, which was equal parts gin, vermouth, and tonic, with a slice of lemon and an olive, all poured over lots of ice. That August in New York, it was all about the ice.

I sipped the drink. It was refreshing. I set it down on a table beside me that was surfaced in white tiles with blue flowers.

"I had a visitor." I watched his face. It didn't tell me anything except he was curious to see what I would say next. "I thought you might know about it."

He frowned, and I thought there was a touch of amusement in it.

"How would I know about your visitor, Harry? Who was it?" His frown deepened a moment, and he added, "I don't spy on you, you know. I trust you."

I gave a small nod. "I know, sir. I didn't think you were spying. I thought you might have sent her."

Now his eyebrows rose high on his forehead.

"Her? And also, why would I do that?"

"I was wondering the same thing." He raised his shoulders an eighth of an inch and shook his head. I went on. "She's Israeli. Her husband and her son were killed at the Kfar Aza Kibbutz massacre on October 7th. Her son was twelve. He tried to defend his mother and his sister with the kitchen knife. They used that knife to decapitate him. Her daughter was fourteen at the time, and they took her. Mohammed Abbasid was in charge of the operation. He was the one who took the girl."

He took a deep breath and gazed out at the vast, black serpent of the Hudson. "And she wants you to bring her daughter back."

"Yeah. And she wants me to kill Abbasid."

He didn't answer. His face was expressionless, like he hadn't even heard me, staring out into space. Eventually he frowned and sighed.

"What did you tell her?"

"I told her I'd bring her daughter back and kill Abbasid."

He shook his head. "You understand Cobra can't be involved."

"Why not? If anyone ever fit the bill, it's Mohammed Abbasid."

"Absolutely. I couldn't agree more, and I would like nothing more than to unleash you on the bastard. But this is Israel we are talking about. They take care of their own, and we would be tramping all over their jurisdiction and possibly spoiling operations they might have been months or even years preparing. We have a very good but very complex relationship with both the Mossad and the IDF. We would be straying well beyond our remit if we started interfering in their affairs. They would be understandably annoyed, and the price we paid could be heavy."

He gave a quick, sudden glance at me and smiled.

"I think we have all learned recently that it is not wise to anger Israel."

"I wouldn't want to, but they have to weigh their priorities. They have a whole nation to protect. I don't have to weigh my priorities. My first overriding priority is Sandra Benzaquen; after that, it's Mohammed Abbasid."

"I can't sanction it, Harry. Clearly I can't stop you either, but I can't offer you any help, and you must be aware that the chance of falling foul of the IDF is high. Not because they would willingly take you out but because they won't know who you are."

I shrugged. "Getting killed by a friend or an ally is no worse than being killed by an enemy." I offered him half of a smile. "If anything, it's worse for the person who kills you. They have to live with it."

The brigadier didn't look amused. He said, "Quite" in a way only the Brits know how and added, "The point is, Harry, if you decide to do this, I can't help you. If there is one thing we don't need now, it's a falling-out with the Israelis. They need us on side and supportive, and we need them."

I went to speak, and maybe he saw a little bitterness in my face because he raised a hand and said, "I am as worried about your personal safety as I am about the diplomatic fallout. You must know by now that I consider you a friend as well as a colleague. If you do this, we have to get it right."

I closed my mouth and nodded. "I have decided to do it. If I get caught, I will make sure they understand it was a private enterprise."

"Have you thought how you are going to approach it?"

"I haven't had much time for planning. She came to see me just before I called you, and I thought I'd discuss it with you before making any plans."

"What made her come to you? How did she know about you?"

"Samuel Cotton recommended me. He was in the IDF Refaim Commando unit, then got seconded to the Mossad. We worked and trained together more than once and became friends. He is a very smart, very dangerous man. Apparently somebody told her to talk to him, and he told her to talk to me."

"Then I assume your first port of call will be to go and have a quiet chat with Sam."

"Yeah, it seems like the best place to start. He might give me some advice on how to stay out of trouble."

He nodded. "Jane and I have been invited to a dinner by Richard and Hester Cavendish at their place on Oyster Bay." I arched an eyebrow, which he ignored. Jane was Colonel Jane Harris of the CIA and the head of Cobra operations. He went on. "I hardly know them, so I imagine they want something from me. Let me have a word with Jane while you make your preparations. The CIA might have intelligence that could be of use to you."

I sipped my drink, and as I set it down, I couldn't stop myself from asking, "They invited you *and* the colonel?"

His eyes might have been chiseled out of ice. "Clearly."

I didn't want it to, but my mouth went right ahead and asked, "Are you and the colonel an item now, sir?"

He took his time answering. "I am going to let it pass this time, Harry, because I know you care about her and you and she have issues you need to resolve. Let me say that no, we are not, as you so quaintly put it, an item. But let me add that if we were, it would be none of your business."

"Yes, sir. I'm sorry."

"Just as your personal, private relationship with her is none of my business until it starts interfering with work."

"Yes, sir."

"Anyway, Harry, I'll talk to her tomorrow and let you know what she tells me. Are you ready for dinner?"

We had dinner and, over coffee and whiskey, the conversation turned to general topics like the importance of Ukraine in a world of increasing drought and famine, the increasingly dominant position of China, and how space was becoming the new high ground.

He sipped his Bushmills, and as he set down his Waterford crystal tumbler, he said, "It was a lesson taught to us repeatedly by Edward III, the Black Prince, Henry V, and Sir Arthur Wellesley, the Duke of Wellington. Choose the high ground, let your enemy come to you, and meet him with a barrage. At the moment, we risk China taking that high ground. The other risk, perhaps a greater one, is that they take the orbit and we take the moon."

"War in space."

He nodded. "So the theory goes. We've actually been at war in space for several decades. Until now it's been a secret, invisible war."

For a moment I thought he was going to continue, but he fell silent.

We had another whiskey, and then I made my way home, unable to shake the feeling that somehow, almost without noticing, I had slipped into a situation where I was well out of my depth.

———

THE BRIGADIER CLOSED the door and stood a moment in thought. Then he crossed the drawing room and moved down a passage to the guest suite, where he knocked softly on the door. The door opened, and the colonel stood in her dressing gown looking up at him.

"He's gone. Do you want a nightcap?"

She nodded and followed him as far as the sofa and the large armchairs. She sat. He mixed her a martini and poured himself another whiskey. As she took her drink from his hand, she asked, "What did he want?"

He sat across from her and crossed his legs, studying her face a moment.

"He's been approached by an Israeli woman. Her daughter is one of the hostages taken by Hamas, just sixteen. She wants Harry to go and get her."

The colonel closed her eyes. "Of course he'll do it."

"Yes, he told me he had decided to do it." He paused a moment, then added, "She also wants him to assassinate Mohammed Abbasid. He was the one who abducted the girl."

"Of course he'll do that." She gave her mouth a humorless, ironic twist. "He'd do that as a free extra on the house." She glanced at the brigadier and frowned. "Cobra can't be a part of this."

"I told him that." He took a deep breath and sighed through his nose. "This business between you and Harry—"

"There is no business between me and Harry, Buddy."

"Come on, Jane. The constant hostility, the fights, the friction, the..."—he hesitated—"the *attraction*. It is affecting our work. It's affecting the organization."

"How?" She snapped the word.

The brigadier raised an eyebrow at her. "Like that, for a start. But worse still, my head of operations, whose skill and expertise I cannot do without, cannot be in the same room with my best operative. That is not a viable state of affairs."

She looked down at her untouched drink, then stared out at the night through the open doors of the terrace.

"I thought he was going to resign," she said half to herself. "I thought he was going to settle down with that doctor in Wyoming. But not even she could stand him."

"Jane." There was reproof in his voice. "That's not fair. He has been through hell, but he's still standing."

"Of course he is." She smiled at the brigadier. "He's indestructible."

"You're in love with him, aren't you, Jane?"

She held his eye for a long moment without answering. Then she gave her head a small shake. "I don't know, Buddy. I have tried for a long time not to be. He stands for everything I most despise in a man."

"But?"

"He is magnetic, primal, brutal, unapologetic... I suppose all that appeals to a woman on a *very* basic, visceral level. But can a woman *love* that? Can a man like that love?"

He grunted. "Well, one way or another, you are going to have to resolve your differences. This is not an acceptable way to run a business." He drew a deep breath. "On a separate matter—"

"Buddy."

He stopped. "Yes, Jane?"

"I'm sorry. I will deal with it."

He nodded and gave a small frown. "Of course. On another matter, after you had retired, while I was waiting for Harry to arrive, I got a call from Richard Cavendish."

She screwed up her brow. "Cavendish? The former president?"

"The very same. He has invited us, you and me, to dine at his house on Oyster Bay tomorrow."

Her frown deepened. "*What?*" She shook her head. "How would he know we had any connection? Why would he send *me* an invitation at all? But especially, why would he send me an invitation through you?"

"I have no idea. It's a little unsettling."

"Is he going to cause us trouble?"

He drained his glass and set it down. "I doubt it," he said. "I have enough on him and his wife to burry them both for the rest of their sorry lives. But he is clearly telling us he knows we are closely connected in some way. And aside from that, it is clearly a last-minute thing. These people issue dinner invitations months in advance. Twenty-four hours speaks of either intimate friendship or very bad manners."

"As the president, he would have known about Cobra, but that was before my time."

"Ex presidents retain a lot of power when they leave office. They keep a lot of unofficial contacts too. That was especially the case with the Cavendishes. They were powerbrokers before they ever came to office, and they have always been very subtle wheelers and dealers. My guess is somebody has told them we work together, and he and Hester probably want a job done."

"That is bad and very dangerous."

He nodded. "I have already started inquires as to who has been talking to him about Cobra. That mouth will be silenced in a way that will send a very clear message. I will also have a private word with Cavendish tomorrow night."

She frowned. "Are you going to execute them?"

He chuckled. "No, Jane. I am not Harry. We take out only approved targets who have committed crimes against humanity. That's the rule, and we stick to it. I will, however, make sure that person loses all security clearance and never works in a position of power again."

She watched him a moment. "You and Harry have so much in common. You are so alike in so many ways. Yet you are so completely different."

For a moment, the brigadier frowned. "Harry is a good man, Jane. I have known him many years. He has huge integrity, and under that somewhat ruthless exterior, he has a great deal of humanity and compassion. And he is not unintelligent."

She smiled. "I know, Buddy. They are some of the things you have in common. But with him, integrity, humanity, and compassion are burning, passionate issues, like everything else, from equality of the sexes to how rare you should have your steak." She gave a small shrug. "With you, it's all just a calm clarity of vision."

The brigadier was a difficult man to embarrass, but right then, all he could manage was, "Well, um..."

The colonel laughed, then smiled with sudden tenderness. "And you are *so* English, Buddy," she said.

He cleared his throat and gave a small shrug. "It's not something I'm ashamed of, despite Sir Kier Starmer's best efforts."

"You shouldn't be," she said. "I like it." She was still smiling. "Never change."

# THREE

A week earlier, at Oyster Bay, on Long Island, Tony La Valle had pulled his Porsche Cayenne across Mill River Road in the dappled shade of the abundant pines, oaks, plane trees, and chestnuts that festooned the neighborhood and entered the Cavendish driveway. It was paved with small red and white cobbles and flanked by tall, dark, narrow poplars. At the end, the drive turned left and opened out into a broad, gravel forecourt. At the center, there was a pond with lilies and goldfish and a couple of weeping willows.

The Cavendish house was painted salmon pink with the window and door frames picked out in white. Tony had always thought that was kind of gay. Obviously he had never said anything. Richard Cavendish was not the kind of man you wanted to upset. Especially as he liked to portray himself as some kind of tough guy from Texas.

La Valle pulled up at the foot of the three broad, shallow steps that led to the front door and grinned privately, looking at the façade. What kind of guy, he asked himself, paints his house salmon *pink?* But then again, he asked himself as he climbed out of his car, what kind of guy marries a woman like Hester Cavendish? She was a woman who specialized in castrating any guy she came across who happened to have any balls. And if half the rumors he'd heard were true, that wasn't just figurative, either.

He climbed the three broad steps, and the door opened before he could ring the bell. It was opened by a guy with gray hair, black and gray striped pants, a gray vest, and a black tailcoat.

"Good morning, Mr. La Valle. Mr. and Mrs. Cavendish are at the pool. They have asked that you join them there."

La Valle chuckled. "Alfred," he said and chuckled some more. "Like Batman. You ever see that?"

The butler, whose name was Crumlin, not Alfred, made no expression but managed to make it look as though he'd caught the whiff of cheap aftershave from La Valle. "Shall I announce you, sir? I believe you know the way..."

"I know the way, Alfred. You go do your butler stuff."

Crumlin's nostrils dilated fractionally, and his eyes glazed with the kind of loathing a conservative father reserves for a son-in-law with pierced ears and nose.

"Thank you sir," he said and withdrew into the shadows of the house.

The entrance hall was about the size of two Manhattan apartments. The floor was tiled in a checkerboard pattern in salmon pink and white marble. La Valle thought it looked just as gay on the floor as it did on the walls. To add fuel to his suspicions, there were statues that looked Greek, and all of them seemed to depict naked or half-naked guys. The ones that weren't guys were women, but those all had dresses.

A staircase, also white and pink marble, rose from the center of the floor and curled to right and left like rams' horns, feeding into a galleried landing that overlooked the hall. La Valle ignored the stairs and made for a set of tall, double walnut doors on the right under the curling stairs. He pushed through them without knocking into a broad, modern drawing room that seemed to be at odds with the rest of the house. There was a large, marble fireplace, low bookcases against the walls, and big, bulky calico sofas and armchairs scattered apparently at random around the room. The far wall was made of giant, sliding plate-glass doors which stood open. Through them, La Valle could see Hester Cavendish stretched out on a deckchair wearing black sunglasses that hid most of her head and a red bikini that hid almost none of her body. The shades, La Valle told himself, were a success. The bikini was a bad mistake.

Richard Cavendish was sitting in a canvas armchair at a white wrought-iron table under a vast parasol. He was reading what looked like a report, which he closed and slipped into an attaché case when he saw La Valle emerge from the house. He watched him approach and waited till he'd stopped walking and stood over the table before smiling.

"Hey, Tony. You look hot and overdressed. Fix yourself a drink." He gestured to a tray on the table that held various bottles and a bucket of ice. La Valle spread his hands and made a little dance, shifting his weight from one foot to another.

"Yeah, thanks, Mr. Cav—"

"Fix me a martini dry, will you? Plenty of ice. And don't drown the gin."

La Valle held up his hands, like Cavendish had pulled a gun on him. "Don't drown the gin. You got it."

Cavendish watched La Valle while he mixed the drinks. When he was almost done, he asked suddenly, "How's the family, Tony?"

La Valle finished mixing the drinks. When he turned to face

Cavendish, his face was a little drawn and had turned a little gray. "Family?" he said.

Cavendish reached out for his drink. La Valle handed it to him.

"You know what I love about my work, Tony? I get to meet so many people in such a wide variety of situations. Take you, for example. How long have you been working for me?"

"Three months."

"First thing you do is buy a Porsche Cayenne. That says something about you—ambitious with a sense of style. Like to impress the girls." He winked.

"I guess so, Mr. Cavendish."

"There's more. You are always alone. You never talk about your wife, your girlfriend, your mother, sister, brother. So you come across as this self-reliant lone wolf kind of character, right? Always on your own." He shook his head, grinned, then laughed. "But I'm thinking, he's Italian, for Christ's sake. All Italians have family! Hell! Even the Mafia is *all about family!* Am I wrong?"

La Valle's voice was small when he answered. "No, Mr. Cavendish. Family is important to Italians."

"*Very* important. A big, noisy, warm family. And you have one! Of course you do: mama, papa, two beautiful sisters, and a younger brother."

La Valle shook his head. Several times he opened his mouth to speak, but no sound came out. Cavendish laughed.

"Oh, come on, Tony! We're family too! Aren't we? Your secret, and your family, are safe with us." He let the word 'safe' hang in the air for a long moment. "We cooperate, we're here to help each other. We're friends. Right? More than friends. Clan. *Family!* Right?"

"Of course, Mr. Cavendish."

"Sit down, Tony. Make yourself at home." He watched Tony sit, then lifted up his sunglasses like a visor on a suit of armor.

"You know what happened to the guy who had your job before you?" La Valle gave his head a small shake. Cavendish went on. "He retired." He pointed roughly in the direction of the bay. "His house is on the corner of Main Street and Shore Road, five bedrooms, two leaded bow windows, open fires in all the bedrooms. I've been there and seen it. I helped him choose it and buy it. His wife loves me." He gave a wolfish grin. "Figuratively, like an elder brother, you understand."

"Right, of course."

"Now he's retired. I'll look after him and his wife until he dies, and I have made provision—trusts—for his kids so if anything happens to him, they are taken care of. I look after my own. I demand a lot, Tony, but in return, I give more than I get. So I want you to believe in me and trust me. I didn't get where I am today, I didn't become President of the United States of America, I didn't become one of the most powerful men in the world, by not taking care of my friends."

"Sure, Mr. Cavendish. I believe in you, and I trust you."

"I am very glad to hear that. You know why? Because I like you." He pointed at La Valle for a second, like he was pointing a gun. Then he wagged the finger a few times. "And I would hate for anything to happen to you or your family. But I have to tell you that, though I am a deeply committed Democrat, I agree with Donald on one key thing. You know what that is? I'll tell you. Revenge. It is not enough in this world to protect yourself. If somebody comes against you, it is not enough to defeat them or get even. You have to seek revenge, to make sure everybody understands you are the meanest son of a bitch in the valley. It is not enough to be respected and trusted. If you want to be on top, people have to fear you."

La Valle had gone ashen. Cavendish pointed at the untouched drink in La Valle's hand and smiled. "You're not drinking."

La Valle drank.

"Now I care about you, Tony. I see you as a kind of younger brother. But I also see that you are at a crossroads in your life. Come with me, down the path I am offering you, and you can look forward to a life of power and wealth for you and your family." He leaned forward and reached out his left hand to grip La Valle's wrist. "We will dine at the same table, you'll bring your girlfriend to dine at my house, I'll pay for your wedding."

He sat back, smiling. "Take the other path, go it alone, without me, and all I see is frustration, poverty, unemployment, loneliness. I know your dad is in the Mafia. And I know you wanted to distance yourself from him. It's why I employed you, and it's why you sought a job with me. Well, not even he will give you a job if you take that path. What path will you take, Tony?"

His laugh was almost shrill. "Oh, I am with you, Mr. Cavendish. Always have been, always will be!"

Cavendish's smile was complacent. "Look at me, Tony. I have a job for you. Do it right, and there is a reward and a bonus at the end of it."

Tony looked him in the eye. "What job, Mr. Cavendish?"

"I need you to kidnap somebody for me. You don't do it yourself. You and I both need plausible deniability, you understand. I need you to arrange the kidnapping so that it cannot be traced to you or me. Do you fully understand that?"

La Valle swallowed hard and nodded. He understood, and he knew how to get it done. "Yes."

"Then understand this also. I will only ever tell you this once. If you fail, I will have your mother killed. Don't fail."

What La Valle wanted in that moment more than anything else on Earth was to take his drink and drain the glass, then pour himself another, stronger one. But his hand was shaking too hard, and he feared if he took the glass, he would spill it and make a fool of himself. Cavendish was watching him carefully.

"Have I made an error of judgment, Tony? Have we got a problem?"

Tony La Valle took a deep, slow breath. In his mind he saw his father's face, the merciless eyes, the unfeeling mouth, the brutal ruthlessness of his gaze that he had wanted to flee from all his life. He knew, as he saw that face in his mind's eye, that he was trapped. Even taking his own life would not be enough. His mother's death would be not just a punishment for him but a warning to others. He was trapped. And in that moment, he had the strange illusion that he was absorbing his father's spirit into himself, in some way becoming his father.

He met Cavendish's eye and held it. He reached out and picked up his glass with a steady hand. He sipped and set it down before answering.

"I doubt you often make an error of judgment, Mr. Cavendish. As far as I am concerned, we don't have a problem. At least, not one I can't take care of for you."

The complacent smile returned to Cavendish's face. He reached down for his attaché case, opened it, and drew out a file an inch thick, perhaps a little more. He tossed it on the table.

"Study it. Make it happen. By the way, all those pages are

photocopies. I haven't touched any of them. You won't get any forensic evidence from them that I have ever handled them or seen them."

"That is the last thing I would look for, Mr. Cavendish. I love my mother, I love my family, and now I love you and Mrs. Cavendish as though you were part of that family."

"Right answer. Go study the file, Tony. Then burn it. Nice of you to drop in. Come over for a barbeque. Soon."

La Valle got to his feet. Hester Cavendish raised her hand and waved at him. He waved back and left.

He made it three hundred yards, to the entrance to the gold course, before he had to pull over. First he started shaking badly, then he started sobbing before he covered his face and rested his forehead on the steering wheel and wept convulsively.

It took about five minutes for the fit of weeping to pass. After that, he blew his nose and wiped his eyes, took his cell from his pocket, and dialed a number. The voice that answered sounded like it had been forged in tobacco, whiskey, and heartlessness.

"Yeah."

"Dad, it's Tony. I need to talk to you."

# FOUR

I dropped Sam Cotton a line in the morning saying I'd be visiting Tel Aviv in a couple of days and would he like to meet up. After that, I had nothing to do. So I spent the day working out and in between sessions reading up on October 7th and in particular the Kfar Aza kibbutz massacre.

I also tried to get what information I could on Mohammed Abbasid, but without access to Cobra's databases, there was not much available. I figured if Cotton had given Miriam my name, maybe he'd be able to get me some kind of intelligence on Abbasid's whereabouts and activities. Who knew? Maybe the Mossad wouldn't be as hostile to me as we expected.

Evening came, and there was no word from the brigadier. It didn't surprise me much. If Richard Cavendish had invited both him and the colonel together, as a couple, it was clear he was playing some subtle game, and the brigadier and the colonel would be fully occupied.

At eleven o'clock that night I made up my mind if I hadn't heard from them by nine the next morning, I'd book my flight and my hotel and go. I may have added what they could both go and do to themselves—and each other—but only under my breath; and it sure as hell didn't affect my ability to sleep. By one-thirty a.m., when my doorbell rang, my eyes were almost growing sleepy.

I pulled on my jeans and went down the stairs. When I opened the door, the colonel was standing on the stoop in a long, dark burgundy dress with a slash up to her hip. She stood staring at me. Her face was drawn and tight. She didn't wait for me to say anything. She brushed past me and snapped, "Close the door."

I followed her into my living room. She turned and stood staring at me. I could see her chest rising and falling.

I scowled. "If this is about what happened in Wyoming, what I said to the brigadier? I already apologized about that."[1]

She didn't say anything. She just stared at me.

I said, "What the hell's gotten into you, Jane?"

"Buddy."

My belly burned hot. A crazy, irrational jealousy smoldered inside me, and I fought to ignore it. I said, "What about him?"

"He's been kidnapped."

"*What?*" I knew as I asked it, it was a stupid question. A voice in my head told me to get a grip. "When and where did this happen? Were you with him?"

She nodded. Her eyes closed, and her bottom lip curled in. I moved to her, took hold of her arms, and guided her to a chair.

"Sit down," I said and went to the sideboard to pour her a glass of whiskey. I handed it to her and sat on the sofa. She tried to talk a couple of times, but each time her face seemed to

---

1. See Harry Bauer 22, *Time to Die*

collapse, and she bit her lip with tears streaming down her cheek.

"Drink," I said. "It will help."

She took a couple of pulls, and it seemed to settle her. Finally she took a deep breath and said, "It happened a hundred yards from the Cavendish house. We were in the Bentley. There were two RAMs across the road. They had the sheriff's department emblem on the side. They were dressed like deputies, and they flagged us down. Denzel stopped—"

"Who's Denzel?"

"The chauffeur. He stopped, and the sheriff came up to his window. As Denzel lowered the window, the sheriff shot him in the head and opened the door. Next thing they were all around us, eight of them. They opened the doors and dragged me and Buddy out. He was fighting like crazy. There were six of them on him in the end. One of them smashed a rifle butt into his head, and they dragged him toward the RAMs."

I frowned. "They let you go?"

"No! I went crazy. I was screaming, scratching and kicking. I was trying to go after Buddy. We were so close to the house. I was screaming for help. In the end, they threw me to the ground and took off in the cars."

She covered her face with her hands. Her shoulders started shaking. "I was useless, Harry. I watched them take him, and there was nothing I could do. I ran to the house, screaming for help."

"Did they talk?"

She frowned at me like I was speaking Greek. "What?"

"The sheriff and the deputies, did they talk?"

Her eyes became abstracted. "No... Yes! Briefly. The sheriff. He shouted at the men who were trying to drag me to the RAMs. He said, 'Come on, leave her.'"

"Think carefully, Jane. What was his voice like?"

She sat quietly for a long time, staring at the floor. Eventually she shook her head. "I'm not sure, Harry. Coarse, harsh, New Jersey, maybe."

"New Jersey." I said it more to myself. "What did Cavendish do?"

"He made a couple of phone calls. The Secret Service showed up in minutes."

"They weren't there already?"

She studied my face a moment, then shook her head. "I'm sorry. I'm not being very coherent. I think I'm in shock." She closed her eyes a moment. "No, they turned up very quickly, like they had been nearby. Then the FBI turned up, with some very senior men. I was questioned repeatedly, and eventually they let me go, and I came straight here, to you."

"Has anybody tried to contact you? Any messages or phone calls?"

She pulled her cell from her purse and checked it. "Nothing."

"You need to check with the senior members of Cobra. You also need to talk to Cavendish and tell him this might have an international dimension, and as a CIA officer, you want to be kept informed of any developments."

She frowned. "What developments?"

"If this had been a hit, they would have shot you and the brigadier when they shot your driver. They didn't. They kidnapped him and abandoned you. That means they want something from the brigadier, or they want something in exchange for the brigadier. They did this right outside Cavendish's house. On the doorstep. That means, one"—I held up my index finger—"they knew you were going to dinner there, and two"—I held up my middle finger—"They knew you were due to arrive at that time. Which in turn means three"—I held up my ring finger—"there is a leak in the Cavendish camp. It might also mean that they want to deal directly with Cavendish. So Cobra—you—needs to pull strings and be kept in the loop."

She nodded, said, "Right," and took a pull on her drink. "He might want to talk to you."

"He doesn't need to know I even exist."

"Right."

"The less people know, the better. Like I said, he has a leak."

"Right." She nodded and said again, "Right."

"Is there anything else you need to tell me? Anything else that might be important?"

"Yes. They were very professional. They were efficient, cold. They knew exactly what they were doing."

"Did you see any of their faces?"

"Yes." She nodded again. "The two who tried to take me. They looked Latino, perhaps Mediterranean or Arab. Dark skin, dark eyes, dark hair. They weren't really tall, average to short."

"Did they speak? Cuss, swear, shout at you, anything?"

"No. They didn't say a word." After a moment, she added, "That in itself is significant, isn't it?"

"Yeah. They are professional. With that kind of discipline, they're probably military. And more to the point, they didn't want anyone to hear their language or their accent."

"You're convinced they're foreign."

I gave a small shrug. "It's a hunch. The brigadier's enemies tend not to be Brits or Americans."

She closed her eyes again. "That's so obvious. I'm sorry. I am not thinking straight."

"Don't worry. It's to be expected. A couple more questions. Then you go to sleep in the guest room."

"I should go home."

"Not after what's just happened. These people are well informed, and they may well know where you live. You stay here until we sort this out."

"Yes, OK."

"Do you know what Cavendish wanted to discuss with you and the brigadier?"

"No, I was as astonished as Buddy was when I was included in the invitation."

I was quiet for a moment, trying to fit things into place, but there were things that didn't make sense.

"When you talk to Cavendish, ask him what he wanted to discuss with you and the brigadier. Don't mention Cobra; see if he brings up the subject. As far as you are concerned, you work for the CIA. You've never even heard of Cobra."

"OK, unless he shows beyond a doubt that he knows."

"Yeah." I nodded. "If he does that, it will raise serious questions and open up a whole new line of investigation."

She finished her drink, and I led her up to the guest room. Last time she had stayed at my place, at my house in Wyoming, she had shared my bed. It was the first time, and apparently the last. We stood a moment in awkward silence in the doorway.

"If you need anything, give a shout."

She gave a small nod. "You'll bring him back, won't you, Harry?"

"Yeah." I gave a humorless smile. "But I may have to blow a few things up in the process."

She laid her palm gently on my chest. "I've complained a lot about you, haven't I? I'm sorry."

"I guess most of the time you had good reason."

She met my gaze and held it. "Blow up whatever you need to blow up, Harry, but bring Buddy home safe."

"I will. Get some rest."

I didn't go straight to bed. I went back down and sat for an hour on the granite step that led down from my French doors to the lawn in my back yard. I stared into the shadows and tried to probe my own mind. Was it a coincidence? A beautiful Israeli woman comes to me and asks me to find her daughter in the ruins of Gaza and bring her home. The next day the brigadier is abducted by professionals who looked 'perhaps Mediterranean or Arab. Dark skin, dark eyes, dark hair. They weren't really tall...'

But the word that kept coming back to me like an alarm bell was 'professional.' I could see her in my mind's eye: 'They were very professional. They were efficient, cold. They knew exactly what they were doing.'

I let my mind scan the Mediterranean. There was only one country there that was noted for the professionalism and efficiency of its troops. On the other hand, if we stayed on the American continent, you didn't have to go farther than Mexico to find highly trained professionals working either for the government or for organized crime.

They were very professional, they had no problem showing their faces, but they were at pains not to be heard. They abducted the brigadier with relative ease—and I knew for a fact that he was not an easy man to abduct—but they couldn't manage the colonel, whose entire military and intelligence career had been spent behind a desk. And—I took a deep breath and blew it out slowly—when forced to abandon the one witness who has seen their faces, these professionals don't shoot her; they simply knock her to the ground and leave her to...

I paused in my thinking. To what? They leave her to do what? To inform whoever conducted the investigation that they were very professional and efficient. They were cold and knew exactly what they were doing? That they were dark-skinned, dark-eyed, dark-haired; that they looked Mediterranean and avoided speaking.

No, I told myself, it wasn't a coincidence. When you lived the kind of lives—when you had the kind of job that the brigadier and I had, you had to expect things like this to happen. So it wasn't a coincidence.

So why did it feel like a coincidence? Why did it feel too much like a coincidence?

When I looked at my watch, it was three a.m. I muttered an obscenity under my breath and called Sam Cotton. It rang four times before he answered. His voice sounded like he was screwing up his eyes.

"Harry? Fucksake, man. You know what time it is?"

"You didn't answer my message."

I heard a sigh and the rustle of sheets as he swung his legs out of bed. When he spoke again, there was a different echo to his voice, like he'd moved to another room.

"I don't like leaving written records, even when they are end to end encrypted."

"We need to talk."

"Not on the phone we don't."

"I need to know."

"You need to know what?"

I thought for a moment. If he was worried about eavesdropping, I had to choose my words carefully.

"You gave somebody my name."

"We'll talk when we meet."

"Wait. What happened to your friend's daughter just

happened to a friend of mine. I need to know if there's a connection."

He was quiet for a long moment. Finally he said, "There might be. That's the best I can do over the phone. There are words like bees, right? You never know when they're going to sting you. Call me when you get here."

He hung up. Words like bees. It wasn't subtle but impossible to mistake his meaning. Buzz words could get you killed.

I had a shower and lay down on the bed without drying myself. I got four hours' troubled sleep. When I got down to the kitchen, the colonel was already there. She'd made coffee and toast but was just sitting, staring at her cup. She looked up as I came in.

"I'll be going back to DC. I'll talk to the board and let you know what they say."

I nodded, sat, and poured myself some coffee.

"I'm flying to Tel Aviv this morning."

"Tel Aviv?"

"You are the only person who knows. Let's keep it that way."

"But I need you here, Harry. We are wasting precious minutes..."

"You want to know where the brigadier is. The answer might be in Tel Aviv. Don't tell anyone where I've gone or what I am doing. Tell me you understand that."

"Yes, I understand, Harry. But Tel Aviv?"

"The less anybody knows right now, the better. Trust me. I'll call you when I get there. Have the Company give you a safe house and have Cobra assign you a bodyguard. If you can disappear, so much the better."

Her eyes and the set of her jaw said she wanted to argue,

but I shook my head at her. I drank my coffee, went up to pack a bag, and fifteen minutes later, I was on my way to the airport with a flight booked to Tel Aviv.

# FIVE

WE LANDED AT BEN GURION AIRPORT AT FIVE A.M. I'd called Sam Cotton from JFK, and he was there to meet me at arrivals. He laughed when he saw me, threw out his arms, and embraced me before holding me at arms' length. "It's been a long time, Harry. Too long, too long."

I agreed, and he grabbed my bag and kept up a stream of energetic small talk all the way to the short term parking lot. The air was cool. The sky was turning pink and gray at the edges, but overhead you could still see a scattering of stars, despite the glow from the airport.

The lights on his Range Rover flashed and bleeped. I climbed in the passenger seat and slammed the door while he got behind the wheel. He fired up the engine and said, "Miriam contacted you?"

"Yeah." I watched the tall lamps and their limpid pools of yellow light reflecting off the few scattered cars as the slipped by. "Is she a friend of yours?"

"No." He glanced at me. "A friend of a friend." He looked out the windshield again as we cruised toward the highway.

After a moment, he started to talk again, like I'd asked him to explain his religion or his political leanings. "You know, in my opinion, Harry, the government is doing the only thing it *can* do. It's stuck in a kind of lose-lose situation." He shrugged as we came off the ramp onto the freeway and took his hands off the wheel so he could spread them in a gesture of helpless self-evidence. "Whatever they do, it's gonna be wrong, right? There's pressure from the States, pressure from Europe, pressure from the United Nations—*a lot* of pressure from the United Nations. Pressure from the families of the hostages, pressure from the people as a whole. Man, Bibi has to balance all of that shit and then make the best decision—because remember there is no *right* decision. He has to make the *best* decision he can for the country in the long term. But at the same time we want—we *need*, as Israelis—to bring those people home."

I watched him and waited. He was driving fast on the almost empty road, heading west toward the coast.

"So what I'm trying to say, Harry, is that sometimes the legitimate needs of the government are not the same as the equally legitimate needs of the people—or some people. Does that make sense?" He glanced at me again. "Does that make any sense at all?"

I was tired. I nodded. "Yeah, I think so. You're telling me there is no official sanction for what Miriam wants me to do."

"Yeah, OK, partly that, but also—" He shrugged again and spread his hands again. "You know? Security is so high at the moment, guys are pulling long shifts, the threat of missiles is always there. What nobody has time for is keeping tabs on one guy who is trying to help a hostage and her mom. You understand what I'm saying? It's what every guy in Israel wishes he could do. And every woman too. We all have better things to do than keep tabs on some ex-SAS Yank. More likely they'll turn a blind eye than get in your way."

"Are you guessing or do you know that?"

He laughed. "You know me, man. I never guess. If you don't know what you're talking about, keep your mouth shut. That's my view."

I smiled. Half to myself. "As I recall, Sam, most of the time you know what you're talking about."

"Right?" Then, half to himself, "If I talk, I know what I'm talking about."

"So are you going to tell me who this friend of a friend is, who sent Miriam to you?"

"No."

"Great. You see, Sam, we have a problem."

"We?"

I nodded. "I think so. Do you remember Brigadier Alexander Byrd?"

"Buddy Byrd, sure. I never met him, but he ran your outfit for a while, right?"

"That's the one. We still work together sometimes in an unofficial capacity."

"Yeah, I heard rumors. So...?"

"The day after Miriam came to see me, he was abducted."

He stared at me, ignoring the road hurtling toward us ahead. "Buddy Byrd has been *abducted?*"

"Yeah. You don't need to tell anyone, by the way..."

"Sure... So how is this *our* problem?"

"I'm not sure. The timing makes me nervous. Also, the guys who took him were dressed like a sheriff and his deputies. There were eight of them."

"That's a lot of deputies."

"Agreed. They stopped the car he was driving in, shot the

chauffeur, knocked him unconscious, and dragged him away to a couple of trucks. The witness who was with him said they were all of Mediterranean or Latino appearance, made no effort to hide their faces but were careful not to speak. They were also very professional. It's a lot of deputies and a lot of contradictions. If they hide their voices, why not their faces? If they're so damn professional, why pull a complicated stunt like that where they *have* to show their faces?" I was silent for a moment, going over my own questions, then added, "To make it even more stupid, they pulled this stunt right outside Charles Cavendish's house at Oyster Bay."

He slowed and turned into Arlozorov Street, moving down toward the coast. It was still dark. One or two desultory cars cruised by with their headlamps on. Sam was frowning hard at the road ahead as we moved through the pools of light from the streetlamps.

"I'm not sure what you're trying to tell me, Harry. You think this was an Iranian proxy attack?" He turned and stared at me hard as we approached Eliezer Peri Street. "You don't think *we* did it! Why the hell would we abduct Brigadier Buddy Byrd, for crying out loud?"

I didn't say anything as we crossed over into Spiegel Park and entered the grounds of the Hilton. He pulled up outside the hotel and sat staring at me for a moment.

"I'll tell you one thing, Harry. If we *had* done it, we'd have done a damn sight better job of it than what you're describing, and you wouldn't be here making stupid, half-assed accusations."

"Relax, will you? I'm not accusing anybody of anything. The Mossad would be the last people on my list of suspects. But—" I sighed and shook my head. "Iranian proxies? They're too busy picking up the pieces back home to make a hit like that. Besides, it's not their style. And getting eight professional jihadists into the States right now would be no easy matter, let alone kitting them out as sheriff's deputies. No, you can smell a jihadist job a mile off. Which leaves a Mexican cartel. But—"

He shook his head and took the words out of my mouth.

"Why would a Mexican cartel go all the way to New York, to Oyster Bay, to abduct Buddy Byrd? A, he's no use to them as a hostage and B, they'd have to have known that he was going to be there that night. How could they have known that?"

"I know, he himself didn't know until about twenty-four hours before. It was a last-minute invitation."

He was still shaking his head. "The Mexicans could abduct a hundred high value targets without leaving southern California. Buddy Byrd is nothing to them."

"I know," I said again and opened the door. "I just wanted to ask you if you knew anything about it. If you'd heard rumors or chatter. It just doesn't make sense whichever way I look at it. And I keep coming back to the timing. Miriam was talking to me in my house in New York about the same time the Brigadier was receiving his invitation to dinner the next day. Don't ask me to explain, Sam. I can't. But it's wrong. It just feels all wrong."

He gazed out of the windshield and grunted. "People like Cavendish don't give you twenty-four hours notice for a dinner invite. They arrange things like that weeks in advance."

"It stinks, Sam."

"OK, listen, I'll make some inquiries. You check in, unpack, get a couple hours' sleep. I'll pick you up at ten. We'll have a late breakfast and discuss Miriam's case. OK?"

He slapped me on the shoulder, I swung down from the cab and went to check in.

In my room, I looked at my watch. It was coming up to six a.m., eleven p.m. in DC. I dialed the colonel's number. She answered on the second ring.

"I'm here. I just checked in to my room. Any news?"

She was quiet so long I thought we'd lost the connection. Finally she said, "Yes."

"What is it?"

"I spoke to Cavendish. I asked him what he had wanted to see us about."

"And?"

"He was familiar with Cobra and our activities from when he was president, and he knew from contacts that I was the head of operations."

"I guess that makes sense. What are you leading up to, Jane? What did he want to see you about?"

"Harry, he wanted to take out a contract."

My mind reeled. For those who knew about Cobra, there was a very precise series of steps that were taken to set up a contract, and they did not involve inviting the director and the head of operations to dinner. On the other hand, Richard and Hester Cavendish had a reputation for taking out contracts on people who got in their way. It had never been proved—they were much too good for that—but those of us in the business knew it was more than a conspiracy theory.

"On who?"

"Ali Hosseini Khamenei."

"*Ali Hosseini Khameni?* That doesn't make any sense at all. The Cavendishes have always had a very close relationship with Iran and especially the leadership."

"I know, they have a couple of billions invested by proxy in Iranian oil."

"Why the hell would they want to kill Khamenei? The man is worth a fortune to them."

"Cavendish's reasoning is that Khamenei, in refusing to negotiate with the current administration, in refusing to back down over nuclear weapons and reach a peaceful accord with Israel, is making it increasingly unsustainable for him and Hester to keep their oil investments. What he wants to do is trigger a change of regime that will be more favorable to their investments."

"Son of a bitch."

"Agreed. He says he has spoken to people in the Company who are willing to facilitate a coup."

I took a deep breath and filed Cavendish away for later consideration.

"What about the brigadier? Has anyone made contact?"

"You're not going to like this. We got a message at Central Intelligence."

"Who's 'we'?"

"Sharp as ever. We is me and my director. We who know about Cobra. We who know Buddy's real value."

"What did it say?"

"The instructions were to take the message to the president. It demands that the US nuke the Iranian nuclear sites. They specify they want MOPs—massive ordnance penetrators—fitted with strategic nuclear warheads. They say the brigadier will be cared for and treated with the greatest respect, but if their demand is not met, he, Cobra, and the involvement of all the heads of state who have used Cobra will be delivered in a file to the Hague."

"Jesus Christ. Who are they?"

"It's a pressure group, Harry. They say they are highly

placed in the Israeli military and government. They call themselves the Guardians of Zion."

I sighed loudly and ran my fingers through my hair. "Again," I said.

"Again? The Guardians of Zi—"

"No, no. I heard you. I mean again, the coincidence which is too much of a coincidence, but there is no apparent connection. Charles Cavendish, a long-standing friend of the ayatollahs, suddenly wants Khamenei taken out, and on the very night he is going to discuss this with you and the brigadier, the Guardians of Zion abduct the brigadier to force the administration into nuking Iran's nuclear facilities. It's too much of a coincidence, but there's no obvious connection. It makes no sense, Jane."

"I know. I agree. There's something else, too." She hesitated, like she was thinking but didn't like what she was thinking. "It's—I don't know how to put this, Harry. It's too improbable."

I'd been standing looking out of the window. Now I moved back and sat on the bed. There was a logic to what she'd said that seemed to cut through everything else.

I said, "From what they said, they are Israeli top brass and politicians. That means they are highly intelligent, educated people. They would know that the threat they are making, however serious, would not be enough to authorize a nuclear strike."

"That's exactly it. They would know that for a demand like that, they would have to go for a much higher value target. What they are threatening could cause a lot of problems for a lot of people, but on the other hand, Cobra is all about plausible deniability. It would not be the end of the world. It certainly would not justify authorizing what would end up being three or four tactical nuclear strikes, which would bring down the condemnation of the entire Arab world—not to mention the United Nations and the wider world."

We were quiet for a long moment. Finally I said, "Who the hell has the brigadier, Jane, and what the hell game are they playing?"

"I don't know, Harry, but I am scared. What are we going to do? The one clue we might have had was their call, but it's left us more baffled than we were before. Where do we go from here?"

I thought about it. "I'm having breakfast with Sam Cotton in a couple of hours. He's going to brief me on the other business, but he told me he was going to make inquiries about the brigadier. Jane, listen to what I am telling you. There are too many parallels and coincidences, especially in timing. There is a connection here. I don't know what it is, but I am going to find it."

"I know you will, Harry."

"I'll keep you posted."

"Thanks."

She was having trouble keeping the sobs out of her voice. She hung up, and I sat staring at the black screen in my hand. After a while I smiled. They would be good for each other. The Odd Couple. There was no doubt he was everything she had ever wanted in a man, and she was just tame enough to give him security and just wild and unpredictable enough to keep him interested. And they were both as solid and reliable as the rising and the setting of the sun. Me and Jane—I shook my head and laughed suddenly. It would never have worked. Not in a million years.

I set my cell to charge, had a shower, lay on the bed, and slipped into a deep, dark, troubled sleep.

# SIX

Brigadier Alexander 'Buddy' Byrd awoke. He opened his eyes and lay staring at the walls and the ceiling. He had a sharp pain in his head, but he was able to ignore it. Long years with the special forces had taught him how to ignore pain. He focused on his immediate environment. The walls were plain and whitewashed, as was the ceiling. There was an air conditioning unit set to twenty degrees Celsius. The bed on which he was lying was comfortable. He became aware that he was wearing pajamas.

He sat up. The room rocked slightly, and a pulse of pain throbbed through his head. For a moment he thought he might vomit, but the nausea passed, and his stomach settled. Against the wall facing him there was a large, free-standing wardrobe and next to it a chest of drawers. Slightly to the right of that a heavy wooden door stood closed.

He carefully swung his legs out of the bed. Facing him now was a window. It was open, but on the outside there were heavy iron bars. Originally, he thought, they would have been to keep people out. Now their purpose was to keep him in.

Over on his right, six feet from the bed was another door. This one stood open, and he could see a set of pine shelves with towels piled on them. An en suite.

He stood, gave the room a moment to settle, and made his way into the bathroom. There was a shower cubicle. He stripped and stood under the water for ten minutes, switching from hot to cold and back again.

After toweling himself dry, he went to the wardrobe and found his clothes hung there along with a number of shirts of his size, a couple of pairs of chinos, and a couple of pairs of shoes. In the drawers he saw two pairs of Wrangler jeans, socks, and undergarments.

The voice of reason in his head told him whoever had brought him here intended him no immediate harm, but neither did they see him leaving in the immediate future.

He dressed and went to stand at the windows. What he could see beyond the iron bars was gray desert. It wasn't golden sand like you see in the movies. It was gray dust, and dotted here and there were small gnarled sage green bushes struggling to survive under an unrelenting, scorching sun.

He tested the bars for strength and found, as he had expected, that they were solid. He turned and tried the door. This he found, to his surprise, opened easily onto a broad passage tiled in terracotta, with the walls lime washed in white. To his left the passage ended with a door that stood open onto a second bathroom. To his right he saw another door some ten to twelve feet from his own, which he took to be another bedroom, and almost opposite that, a broad arch framed in raw brick. He approached and stepped through.

He found himself in a large room that was almost square. Opposite him was a heavy wooden door which was closed.

Beside it to the left, maybe six or seven feet away, was a tall window, floor to ceiling. Wooden shutters stood open, allowing light to stream through glass panels, forming checkered patterns on the red terracotta tiles on the floor. This window too had iron bars.

There was a large, overstuffed beige sofa with its back to that window, a couple of matching armchairs, and a rustic open fireplace. There was a bull's hide on the floor and a couple of bookcases. One held a tray with whiskey, brandy, gin, and vermouth. A small dining table with four chairs stood to one side.

On the right there was a breakfast bar enclosing a kitchen.

He crossed the room and tried the door. It didn't budge. A careful inspection of the house revealed only one camera, and that was over the front door. He found the kitchen stocked with food, fruit juice, and coffee.

It was only after he had made coffee and toast that he noticed the small television in the corner of the living room. There was a white square envelope resting against it. It bore the legend *Watch Me*. Inside he found a DVD which he slipped into a small DVD player that was connected to the TV.

He sat with his coffee and watched.

It showed the same living room. The camera moved slightly to center on a chair. Then a body appeared from off screen, crossed the room, and sat looking at the camera. It was a man in military fatigues. He had a ski mask pulled down over his face with eye-holes cut into it. His voice, when he spoke, was distorted. There might have been an accent, but he could not be sure.

"Brigadier Byrd, you are welcome to our house. We intend you no harm. We understand you will be annoyed and inconvenienced, and we are sorry for that, but it is not our intention to cause you serious pain or injury. We have provided here all that you will need for your immediate comfort, and we hope not to have to keep you too long. We have the greatest respect for you, Brigadier, and for the work you do. Unfortunately, faced with betrayal by our allies and partners, we are left with no choice but to take this action. Iran must be stopped. There is no other alternative. You will be provided with food, drink, and care."

The man stood and walked back behind the camera. The video ended, and the brigadier sat sipping his coffee and staring at the empty chair. He ran the narrative through his mind again, highlighting those things that seemed important:

"Our house." Was that serious? Did the house actually belong to them? It looked clean and inhabited. Had they occupied it while the owners were away? If it was genuinely theirs, he could easily trace them once he got out. It would also make them amateurs, and yet their attack had been slick and professional. He filed away the thought and moved on.

"We understand you will be annoyed and inconvenienced, and we are sorry for that." It sounded all wrong. It was again the wrong language. It was like a supermarket apologizing for having to close due to causes beyond their control. He gave a small, private wince and scratched his head. It was like sitting with your bank manager as he explained that the IRS was causing problems and he couldn't stop them. Again he filed away the observation and moved on.

"We have the greatest respect for you, Brigadier, and for the work you do." This was more interesting. Because it shrank the suspect pool down to a very small number of people within an even smaller number of groups. It was not the statement itself —that they respected what he did. That could be a lie. It was the fact that they *knew* what he did. Very, very few people knew what he did.

In his mind, he set a list rolling with the names and faces of all those who knew of his role in Cobra. To that he applied the filter that they spoke like apologetic bank managers. He allowed his unconscious mind to work on that and moved on to the final point.

"...faced with betrayal by our allies and partners..." and "...Iran must be stopped. There is no other alternative..."

The abduction had occurred in New York, outside the home of a former president of the United States. His own English nationality was not the issue here. The allies and partners in question were not British allies and partners but American ones. And the only allies and partners of America who could complain of having been betrayed recently were the Israelis. That would explain the slick professionalism of the abduction. It would explain the comfortable conditions. It could even almost explain the bizarrely formal nature of the language.

Almost.

But this would not be the Israeli government. On the face of it, the current administration and the Israelis were cooperating. No, this would be a splinter group who felt the US had not finished the job, and Iran was still mere months away from making a nuclear device.

He rose and went to the window again. That desiccated, gray desert, he told himself, could well be southern Israel.

———

LA VALLE HAD BOUGHT himself a new suit from Armani. He was wearing it as he sat in Richard Cavendish's study sipping a glass of the Macallan which he knew cost at least five hundred bucks a bottle. He was leaning back in a burgundy leather chair which Cavendish had just told him had been in his great-great grandfather's study in Texas as two thousand Federal troops marched into Galveston in 1865. Cavendish now sat opposite him, toasted him, and sipped.

"I have to say, La Valle, I am very pleased with the way you managed that job. I could not have asked more from a seasoned pro. Now, normally, I would not want to know any details about a job like this, and I would ask you to remember that in the future. But this case is a little special. So where is our guest right now?"

La Valle gave it some thought before answering. "Let me put it like this. An acquaintance of one of my uncles owns a house out in the desert, about thirty miles from the Egyptian border, near the Ramat Hovav power station, in southern Israel."

"So what happens if somebody traces the ownership of the house?"

"Nothing. The house has been unoccupied for a long time. It's not a place most people would want to live. A long time ago they thought about making some kind of oasis out there with a pool and a big shady garden. But they never got around to it."

"Jews."

"Right. My uncle says they make good lawyers. So the house has been empty for a while. Anyone could force the locks and use it."

What about fingerprints, DNA...?"

"Latex gloves and bleach. Two guys with a lot of experience cleaned the place top to bottom. The only prints or DNA will be the guest's."

"OK, Tony. I am very happy. Now I have to tell you because I like you and I'm looking out for your career. I have recorded this conversation, but the microphone is triggered by your voice. So my part of the conversation was not recorded, you understand? It's not that I don't trust you. It's that you can never have too much insurance. We good?"

La Valle smiled. "Sure, Mr. Cavendish. I am learning a lot from you."

"That is the right attitude. I'm proud of you. So what I want next from you, is you arrange for the guest to be killed. Somebody has to go there and shoot the bastard."

"Consider it done."

"Wait a couple of days. And whoever does the job needs to use a BUL M-5."

"A BUL M-5?"

"Unregistered, obviously. And the weapon must be found at the scene."

"I will do it exactly as you say, but an Israeli pro ain't gonna leave his gun behind."

"Unless it is left as a message. The registration filed, all the prints wiped. It will basically be saying, you didn't listen. This is what you get."

"Man."

"You're playing in the big league now, Tony. High stakes and ruthless players."

"Are we looking for a war with Israel?"

Cavendish laughed. "No! They'd probably win!" He laughed some more. "No, we just want to shift them off their pedestal a bit. There is growing anti-Semitism, Tony, we know that. But there is also a backlash against that. So we want to weaken that backlash. Some of us would rather be friends with the Arabs than the Jews, Tony. The Arabs have more oil, and they don't worry so much about democracy. Right?"

"Right."

Cavendish drained his glass and stood to refill it, indicating with his finger that La Valle should finish his drink. He took La Valle's glass and walked to the sideboard, where he refilled both, speaking over his shoulder.

"You've probably heard talk about how the United States was established as a republic, not a democracy. In fact, it was established over time as a republic with democratic features, right back when the first democracies were emerging in the West."

"Tell the truth, I'm not much of a political animal, Mr. Cavendish."

"That's fine. I just don't want you to get scared by some of the things I say from time to time." He handed La Valle his drink and laughed. "I *was* a democratic president, after all. But the fact is, Tony, democracy is a failed experiment. And what more and more people in positions of political power are realizing is that a benign dictatorship which takes care of its people is what we all really want."

"A benign dictatorship?"

"Sure, a state that provides its people with national welfare and medical care from cradle to grave, an education, a job, even a home. So all *they* need to do is enjoy life! What could be better?"

La Valle grinned. "Well, it does sound pretty good. But how do you do something like that?"

"You put government in the hands of the really smart guys, like me!" Cavendish threw back his head and laughed again. "You generate wealth through labor, and you share that wealth sixty-forty. Sixty percent for the state and forty percent so the people can cover their basic needs."

"Well, I'll take your word for it, Mr. C. I just hope you ain't gonna take back sixty percent of that bonus you gave me!"

"Oh, no, Tony." Richard Cavendish stopped laughing. "That is for them. *We* do the serious stuff, and we reap the rewards."

# SEVEN

My phone jangled my nerves and dragged me violently out of a nightmare. I sat up and grabbed it from my bedside table.

"Yeah?"

"Did I wake you?" It was Sam Cotton.

"Yeah. Give me ten minutes. I'll be down."

I stuck my head under the cold shower for two minutes, dried my hair, and changed my clothes. Then I went down and found Sam in the lobby reading a newspaper. He stood as I approached and gave me a complicated hand shake.

"Come on, I want to introduce you to somebody."

I followed him outside where he had a dark Grenadier waiting. He climbed behind the wheel, and I got in beside him. We took off at speed, and he didn't speak until we'd joined Highway 4, headed south toward Gaza.

"You're a smart guy, Harry." He nodded like he was agreeing with himself and glanced at me. "I remember, you were always smart. You think quick. I liked that in you."

"Gee, thanks. I think I'm going to blush."

He chuckled. "It's why I told Miriam to go talk to you. Now I am going to ask you a question. I'm going to ask you *two* questions. Do you think—this is question number one—do you think there is anybody on this planet that the IDF or the Mossad need to ask for help in order to get a job done?"

I arched an eyebrow at him. I could see he was serious, so I thought about it. "On the face of it," I said, after a moment, "obviously not."

"See you're smart. '*On the face of it.*' Nobody has more skill or experience than us, right?"

"What's your point? There's obviously a 'but' or 'however' coming."

"Give me a minute. This is my second question: Can you think of a single special operations outfit on that planet that is coming under closer scrutiny than the IDF units are right now?"

I shook my head. "No."

"So we face a daily existential threat, we have this intense scrutiny from the whole world, and *a lot* of people are just waiting for us to do something wrong so they can pounce and accuse us of human rights violations, atrocities, you name it. And right now, with the problems in Gaza and Mr. T and his Nobel Peace nomination doing what he's doing to transform Gaza into the new Riviera, we have to be very, very careful not to rock the boat."

"Right. I get that. So again, what's your point?"

He didn't answer right away. The highway ahead seemed to be populated by stationary cars as we hurtled along the inside lane. I glanced at the speedometer and saw he was doing a hundred and twenty miles per hour.

"You in a hurry?"

"Always. We have somebody waiting for us." He sucked his

teeth, took a deep breath, and said, "So while the politicians talk, we, fathers, sons, and brothers, wait and pray that what's left of Hamas is treating the hostages humanely because they are now as keen for peace as we are. Only they're not, but we hope and we pray."

I had started nodding slowly. "So what you need," I said as I watched an Audi go Doppler backwards on my right, "is a guy who will do what you want to do but allow you to invoke plausible deniability."

He grinned at me. "See? Smart."

"You kind of hinted at this earlier."

"Right, but there is more to it than that. I'm going to let the colonel explain it to you, though."

I studied his face a moment. He kept his eyes firmly on the road.

"The colonel?"

"Colonel Ben Gordon."

"*Gordon?*"

"Yeah. His father was Scottish, but his mother was Jewish. He's a great guy. You'll like him. He was in your outfit for a couple of years."

"The SAS?"

"Yup."

Shortly after that, we came off the highway and wound down a series of dusty roads toward Zikim Beach. Before we got there, he turned off and entered a kind of suburban cluster of houses set among sand dunes. We pulled up outside a house which was pretty much like all the other houses, and Sam smiled at me. "Let's go, pal."

We swung down, and I followed him through a white picket fence and down some crazy paving across a dry, yellow lawn to a cheerful red door. He rapped it with his knuckles three times fast and then three times slow. After that, he put a key in the lock and opened the door. As he stepped through, he shouted, a little louder than was necessary, "*Boker Tov*, Colonel! It's Sam, with our friend!"

I followed him into a small entrance hall. A flight of stairs rose to an upper floor immediately on the right. Ahead of us, a narrow passage led past the stairs to a kitchen and before that an arch that gave onto a living room. In that archway stood a man. He wore jeans and a khaki shirt. He must have been six foot six with powerful shoulders and very short hair turning to gray. He had what looked like a Sig Sauer in his hand, but it was pointed at the floor. When he spoke, his voice was quiet and deep.

"*Shalom.*"

He holstered his weapon and stepped forward with a hand like a small barbell held out in front of him. He surprised me with a smile. "I am Colonel Benjamin Gordon."

We shook. "Harry Bauer."

"We are here to break the law, Harry. I hope you understand that. If you want out, now is the time, and no hard feelings."

"I don't want out, Colonel. I want to hear what you have to say."

He led us through to a small living room with a shabby sofa and two chairs arranged around a small, melamine coffee table. He gestured to a chair, took the other, and Sam took the sofa.

The colonel said, "Miriam Benzaquen has employed you to rescue her daughter."

It was a statement, not a question, but I shook my head. "No. She hasn't employed me, and I am not taking any money from her. She asked me to do it, and I agreed."

He was quiet for a moment, staring at me, then nodded.

"Normally, as I am sure you are aware, we would not welcome that kind of interference in our affairs. It is dangerous and can lead to innocent people getting hurt, not least the hostages themselves."

"I understand that. I also gather you are making an exception in this case."

He smiled somewhere between ruefulness and irony. "Not exactly, Harry. Let me explain. When we started the campaigns against Hamas, Hezbollah, and Iran itself, one of the first things we did was to take out as much of the leadership as we could, and we were quite successful."

"It was impressive."

"We took out Yahya Sinwar, one of the main leaders of Hamas and the main organizer of the October 7th massacres. But one of his right hand men has so far escaped justice—"

I arched an eyebrow at him. "Mohammed Abbasid."

He frowned. "You know about him?"

I looked at Sam. "Do you guys have this whole thing orchestrated?" I turned back to the colonel. "Miriam mentioned his name. He's the guy who took her daughter."

He grunted softly. "We want him executed."

"That's not a problem. But you didn't bring me here to the border with Gaza just to tell me that. Sam could have told me this at the hotel."

"No, there is more."

"What more?"

"We will help you in what ways we can. I am going to ask a lot of you, but no more than I would ask of myself or any Israeli."

"What?"

"Mohammed Abbasid goes everywhere with at least four lieutenants. They have children's blood on their hands."

"I'll take them out too."

He hesitated and took a deep breath. "And we have reliable intelligence that there are four more girls with Sandra. They are all around fifteen, and they are at very high risk. Bring them back home to us."

I stared at him for a long moment. "Is one of them yours?"

He gave his head a small shake. "No, Harry. If one of them were mine, I would have gone in for her already. These girls are daughters of Israel, and they need to come home."

"That's five girls and me on my own. That's fine, but the risk to them is increased exponentially."

He nodded. "We have debated this over and over. We end up going in circles. But the bottom line is that the risk to them in escaping is no greater than the risk if they stay. Especially if the negotiations fail. The truth is, every one of us knows that those girls may already have been raped and murdered. You should know that too."

I felt the slow, hot coals of rage in my belly.

"What help can you provide me with?"

"More than you might expect, Harry. We have reliable intelligence about where they are being held. We can assist you in getting in, we can assist you with hardware, and when the time comes, we can assist you in getting out. We can't extract you, obviously, but we can distract them."

From where I was sitting, through the window I could just make out the blue gleam of the Mediterranean beyond the sand dunes. I gazed at it while I let everything he had told me unfold in my mind. Finally I asked, "Who is 'we,' Colonel?" I turned to look at him. "You wouldn't be the Guardians of Zion, would you?"

The colonel frowned. "We are a small group who believe it would be naïve to take Hamas, Hezbollah, or Iran at their word. A ceasefire to these psychopaths is little more than a chance to regroup and plan their next atrocity. We don't waste time with glamorous names, Harry. Who are the Guardians of Zion?"

I wondered for a moment whether to tell him and saw no reason not to. I had known Sam for years, and I had trusted him with my life. As for the colonel, I wasn't so sure, but my gut told me he was solid.

"Within twenty-four hours of Miriam coming to see me, my friend and old commanding officer was abducted. It was a slick, professional operation with a few odd features. The group claims to be called the Guardians of Zion and are demanding that the United States nuke Iran's nuclear facilities."

He managed to snort and look troubled all at the same time. "It's ridiculous. They abducted a British officer nobody has ever heard of to coerce the President of the United States? What happened? It was the weekend and there were no senators available?" He made the face of extreme skepticism and shook his head. "No, Harry. Believe me, you will find few people in the Israeli military and intelligence community who would not agree with the sentiment. Iran is enriching uranium, and they are close to achieving the ability to make tactical weapons. That is an existential threat to Israel. It is also a threat to Egypt, Saudi Arabia, Jordan, Syria, and Lebanon, not to mention Cyprus and Gaza. And if it was any other nation on Earth, we would feel confident that they would not strike with a nuclear weapon. But Iran is Shiite, and most of our neighbors are predominantly Sunni, and the ayatollahs are insane enough to be willing to take out the whole area for the greater glory of Allah.

"So yeah, you would find support for the use of low-yield

tactical atomic strikes on Iran's nuclear facilities. But if we were going to pressure the United States, in the first place we would use some kind of method that would work; second, we are aware we would have to pressure a lot more people than just the president; and third, Harry, we wouldn't bother because we know damned well he is not going to authorize a nuclear strike on Iran. It's just not going to happen. If anybody nukes Iran, it will be us. We don't need the US to do it for us."

He turned and looked at Sam. "Is this Buddy?"

Sam nodded.

He seemed to think for a moment. "I'm going to make inquiries." He glanced at me. "I know Buddy. He's a good man. I'm going to look into this, but I can tell you, Harry, if we were behind this, you would not know about it, and we would get a result. Not this result."

"Thanks."

"I'll keep you in the loop. Quid pro quo."

"I appreciate that."

"Before that. Do we have an agreement on the rescue operation and the execution?"

"We have an agreement. I will get the girls and bring them home. While I am at it, I will take out Mohammed Abbasid and his men. I need names and photographs and any other intelligence you can give me."

"We will provide everything we have, plus ordnance, don't worry about that. Mr. Cotton will take you back to your hotel. I suggest you do tourist things for the rest of the day, and at about six p.m., Mr. Cotton will collect you and take you to have dinner."

I drew breath, but he raised a hand. "Before you go, Harry. Please give me the precise details of Buddy's abduction."

I filled him in from beginning to end, including the

messages the colonel had told me about, and he sat for a long time just staring at me, like he was trying to read in my face if I was lying or not. Finally he said, "Ham-fisted, incompetent, ill-informed and yet slick and professional in the execution. Planned by an idiot and executed by experienced professionals."

I grunted. "That is nicely put. It seems to sum it up."

He stood. "I'll see you this evening."

A moment later, the door closed, and he was gone, like he'd never been there.

Sammy got to his feet. I watched him a moment. He said, "Shall we go?"

"Sure."

I got to my feet, though I had no intention of doing tourist things for the rest of the day. Miriam Benzaquen had given me her address in Tel Aviv on her pretty lavender visiting card when she came to see me in New York, and I intended to drop in and say hello. I also intended to ask her how come there were so many coincidences surrounding her daughter's abduction. The timing of the attack on the brigadier and the colonel I could just about swallow—with difficulty. The Guardians of Zion, Colonel Ben Gordon and his friends, the hit on Mohammed Abbasid and his four pals, and Sandra Benzaquen and the four other girls with her were all just four or five coincidences too far. I wanted answers, and Miriam was going to give them to me. Even if I had to take her out to do tourist stuff and eat ice cream on the beach.

# EIGHT

She had an apartment on the twelfth floor of a block overlooking the sea on the corner of Retsif Herbert Samuel Street and Ha'Rav Kook. I was approaching from the north along the coast road in my new rental, a generic Franco-German-Niponese Citroen-Wagon, looking for a space to park. I found one maybe a hundred yards from her block, pulled in, and killed the engine. I was about to climb out when a car parked directly outside her block caught my eye. I sat back and frowned.

The Ineos Grenadier is a great machine. It's the closest thing to a true old Land Rover: built like a tank with lots of power and just enough comfort to keep going without falling asleep. It's a great truck, but it is not a common one. You don't see a lot of them on the roads. It's a connoisseur's car, and they don't make many in a year. To see two in a single day would be unlikely, but that was exactly what I had just done: I had just seen my second Grenadier of the day right outside Miriam Benzaquen's apartment block.

I closed the door again, slouched back in my seat, and blew air through my teeth. "Have I?" I said quietly to myself. "Or is it the same Grenadier, and I am seeing it for the second time?"

I waited fifteen minutes, and then the answer came: It was the same Grenadier, and I was seeing it for the second time. The big glass doors of the apartment block opened and, only slightly to my surprise, Colonel Benjamin Gordon emerged. He skipped down the steps, climbed into the truck, and drove away at speed.

Sam had collected me at the airport in a Range Rover, but he'd collected me from the hotel in that car. Now the colonel was using it to visit Miriam at her private apartment. What did it mean? Did it mean anything? Or was I reading too much into an innocent event? I decided I wasn't, but that didn't help much. I still didn't know what it meant. After a few minutes, I got out and made my way to Miriam's apartment block. I rode the elevator to the top floor and rang her bell. She opened it after only a few seconds, smiling like she expected it to be somebody else. When she saw me, she froze. I smiled.

"Hello, Miriam."

She managed "Mr. Bauer" but then froze again. "I'm sorry. I wasn't expecting..."

"You gave me your address. I thought you'd like to be put up to speed before I go in. Perhaps I should have phoned you to let you know I was coming. Is this a bad time?"

"No! Heavens! Where are my manners?" She tried a laugh but didn't do a great job. "Please come in."

It was a nice apartment. Spacious and airy with lots of light. She showed me into a broad living room with comfortable modern furniture, a sweeping view of the ocean through glass doors onto a balcony, and broad windows.

She gestured me to a suede armchair. "Please sit down, Mr. Bauer. Can I offer you a drink?"

I gave my head a small shake. "I won't keep you. I just wanted to update you as to where things stand right now and also ask you a couple of questions that would be helpful to me."

She sat on the sofa, and I sat opposite her. I was momentarily distracted by how large and dark her eyes were. She was smiling, and that was distracting too. It struck me suddenly that she had no idea just how attractive she was. That made me return the smile with feeling.

"I saw Ben as I was coming in." Her eyes seemed almost to glaze for a moment. "Benjamin Gordon, the colonel." She gave a small nod and spoke almost in a whisper. "Yes."

It was confirmation that she knew him and he had been here. It was enough, for now at least.

"Miriam, what can you tell me about the Guardians of Zion?"

Her eyebrows went high on her forehead, and she gave a small laugh.

"Nothing. It sounds like a children's television animation."

"Nobody from the Guardians of Zion has approached you or contacted you?"

"No. I have never heard of them."

I nodded. "OK, that's fine. Miriam, before I go on, I want you to be absolutely clear that I am going to go and get your daughter back, safe and sound, and I am going to take care of all the business we talked about. OK?'

She nodded. "Yes, of course. Thank you."

"But there are a couple of things I need to clear up first because they could affect your daughter's safety when I bring her out. So help me get this clear in my head, Miriam. Was it in fact Ben who recommended me?"

She hesitated just a moment too long. "I discussed the problem with Ben. He told me to talk to Sam."

"Why?" I asked her very gently, but it made her falter. She said, "What?"

"Why did he suggest Sam? I have known Sam for many years. He's a great guy, he has many skills, and he was a good soldier. But search and rescue and extraction were never among his skills. I was wondering why Ben recommended him. He must know a dozen guys better qualified than Sam."

She looked like she was about to cry but was fighting really hard not to show it.

"I don't know. Is there a problem, Mr. Bauer? He said Sam had many connections, and he might know someone with the right skills."

"Oh, I see. No, there is no problem at all. Please call me Harry. If I am going to get your daughter back from Hamas, I think that makes us friends. You said that to me in New York, remember?"

She smiled and nodded and seemed to relax. "Of course. Harry."

I stared at the floor, struggling with the questions. Her vulnerability was palpable, but it was also becoming increasingly clear to me that I was being used in some kind of game, and as much as Miriam Benzaquen touched me, I was not going to be a pawn in anyone's scheme. I looked up, and she held my gaze.

"You have known Ben for a long time, haven't you, Miriam?"

"Yes."

I could feel my mind reaching out, almost as though I

could reach inside her mind for the truth I was looking for. And something in her eyes told me she wanted to open up to me but couldn't.

"Miriam, you, Sam, Ben, you are holding something back from me." She closed her eyes and tried to speak but couldn't. I said, "Is Sandra still alive?"

Her answer was barely a whisper. "I don't know."

"I am being sent on an execution mission, aren't I?"

"You said you'd kill him for me. You promised."

"I will, Miriam. But please remember, you also made a promise to me." I paused a moment, then I added, "I am risking my life to bring back your daughter. I think I deserve the truth."

"Mr. Bauer—Harry—please. All I want is my daughter back."

She covered her face with her hands and went very silent and very still. When she removed them, her cheeks were wet, and I could see the tears flooding her eyes.

"I'm sorry, perhaps I should have told you I wasn't sure, for certain, that she was still alive. I was wrong, but it's a difficult thing to admit. And I really thought you would know that with Hamas, nothing is ever certain. It just never crossed my mind..." She trailed off, then shook her head. "Please don't go back on your promise."

I raised a hand like I was trying to slow her down. "Miriam, take it easy. I am not going to go back on any promises. All I am asking is to understand what's going on. Did you approach the colonel, or did he approach you?"

She searched my face. "Does it make any difference? They committed these crimes. They deserve to die. If there is a one percent chance Sandra is alive, she deserves to be rescued. We should at least try, shouldn't we?"

I nodded throughout her speech. When she'd finished, I said, "Mohammed Abbasid deserves to be executed, and Sandra deserves to be rescued. No argument from me. But, Miriam, I do not deserve to be played or used as a pawn in somebody else's game. Like I said to you, if I am going to risk my life to save your daughter and bring Abbasid to justice, I deserve to know the truth. Am I being used?"

Her cheeks colored. She placed her palms together and clasped them between her knees. It took a while. I waited quietly, and eventually she said it.

"He came to me. We have known each other for years. He knew what had happened to my family in Kfar Aza. He was deeply opposed to the ceasefire. He believes we should go to Gaza and exterminate Hamas, then go into Lebanon and exterminate Hezbollah. Finally, he believes we should use tactical nuclear devices in Iran to stop their enrichment program." She still had her hands clasped between her knees, but she raised her shoulders half an inch. "When they agreed to the ceasefire, he was furious because it meant we could not go and get the remaining hostages. And we know what Arabs are like when they negotiate. It can go on for months or years. And all that while, he said, they are regrouping and rearming."

"He has a point."

"So he came to me and told me there was a chance we could have someone go in to get at least my daughter, perhaps more people, and strike a hard blow at the Hamas leadership by killing Abbasid and his right-hand men."

"But it couldn't be an Israeli action. It had to be plausibly deniable."

"Yes."

"So you spoke to Sam, who had a wide range of contacts, and asked him if he could recommend anyone. He recommended me, because he knew about the Al-Landy massacre and what I had done afterwards."

"Benjamin spoke to Sam. Then they asked me to go and see you in New York."

I eased myself back in the chair and took a deep breath. I let it out slowly as I gazed at the ceiling. It made sense. Everything she said made perfect sense, and it squared with what I knew of Sam and what my gut told me about Colonel Gordon. But there was a weakness. It didn't explain everything.

"Who else have you discussed this with?"

"Nobody!" She frowned. "Benjamin was very insistent on that point. It had to be between us four, and nobody else could know. There was too much at stake."

I believed her. But if what she said was true, how could I explain the brigadier's abduction? How could I explain the synchronized timing, and the underlying aim to nuke the Iranian nuclear facilities? It was too much of a coincidence that Colonel Gordon had that very thing on his wish list, and it was the core demand from the Guardians of Zion.

The truth was, if your nation, which was the size of New Jersey, faced the daily threat of extermination by a country with uranium enriching plants hidden in a vast, mountainous desert, you would probably find quite a lot of people in favor of deploying a couple of low-yield nuclear devices. The difference here was that in temperament, skill, and professional standing, Colonel Benjamin Gordon was the kind of guy who would not just talk about it. He would try to make it happen.

I sighed and stood.

"Thank you, Miriam. I'll be in touch in the next few days."

She stood too and approached me, reaching for my arm. "It is not my intention, or our intention, to use you or play games, Harry. I am sorry if it seems that way. What I said to you in the beginning was the truth. It has not changed. I am so grateful to you. You must know that."

"I know, Miriam. I know that." For a moment, I was about to tell her about the brigadier and the demands that had been made. Maybe if I had, things might have unfolded differently. As it was, all I did was smile. I reached out and took hold of her shoulder. "All I ask is that if you hear anything—even just the name—of the Guardians of Zion, you contact me and let me know immediately."

"Of course."

"I'm going to see Colonel Gordon in a while. I'll tell him about our conversation, so please feel free to tell him I came here. The last thing I want," I said with perhaps more warmth than I intended, "is to put you on the spot."

Her eyes roved my face for a moment. Her expression made me feel good.

"Thank you," she said and placed a very gentle kiss on my cheek.

I went back out to the car. I glanced at my watch and made my way slowly back to the hotel to have some lunch and a good think. Even with Miriam's explanation, it didn't fully make sense. Which meant there were things she didn't know or wasn't privy to.

At six o'clock I'd be meeting up with Colonel Gordon again, and something told me if anyone was privy to what was going down, it was him. So maybe it was time for me and him to have a heart to heart. If he was going to use me, he ought to know exactly who he was using and just how dangerous this pawn could become.

Before firing up the Honda-Megan Standardmobile, I called the colonel.

"Harry, are you OK?"

"I'm fine. Any news?"

"Yeah, the brigadier must have had some pretty heavy strings he could pull. The president has convened a meeting with the directors of the CIA and the FBI as well as military intelligence. He has also summoned the Israeli ambassador. They are keeping it tightly under wraps. It hasn't hit the news yet, but if and when it does, things are going to get messy. Have you got anything?"

"I don't know. More small coincidences but nothing concrete. I might know more tonight. I'll keep you posted." I hesitated a moment. "Listen, before you go. Do you know anything about a Colonel Benjamin Gordon with the IDF?"

"No. I never heard of him, why?"

"The brigadier never mentioned him?"

"No."

"Can you make inquiries at the Company?"

"Sure, why?"

"I'm not sure. We'll talk later."

I hung up and sat staring at the windshield without seeing it. The president had convened a meeting with the directors of the CIA and the FBI, as well as Military Intelligence. This mild-mannered Brit who wasn't even part of the American military had half of DC's military, intelligence, and political elite panicking because he had been abducted. Not only that, his abductors believed he was valuable enough to the president that he would nuke Iran to save him. Maybe they were right, after all. Maybe the very reason the brigadier was able to run Cobra and keep it so well hidden was precisely because he pulled so much weight—or so many strings—behind the scenes.

And all of that raised an important question: He was a private man; few people knew him, fewer still knew him well.

So who knew him well enough to know he pulled *that* kind of weight? The colonel and I knew him as well as anyone, and we'd had no idea.

So that meant his abductors came from a very small pool indeed.

# NINE

Sammy Cotton showed up at six sharp. He was waiting for me in the lobby, and I followed him out to where the Grenadier was parked. I took my time having a good look at the vehicle and the license plates. It was a dark military green with running boards and a no-BS design reminiscent of the best Land Rovers.

"Nice truck, Sammy. What is it, the 1924 Limited Edition?"

He arched an eyebrow at me, said, "Yup," climbed behind the wheel, and slammed the door. I continued my inspection before climbing in the passenger seat.

"How much does one of these babies set you back? They're about ninety grand, aren't they?"

He shrugged as he pulled out. "I don't know. It's not mine."

"Colonel Gordon's?"

He eased into the traffic on Ha Yarkon and turned south.

"That's a lot of questions about a car, Harry."

"It's a rare car. You don't see a lot of them around."

"What's your point?"

I studied his face a moment. He glanced at me, then back at the road.

"I'd like to know what the hell you, Gordon, and Miriam are doing. I'm happy to do the job—both jobs—but you keep trying to play me like a pawn and I'll shove your head so far up Gordon's ass you'll be able to look through his eyes and tell me how it feels to be a colonel with an asshole shoved up his ass."

For a moment he looked mad. Then he threw his head back and roared with laughter. "That's good," he said. "That's funny."

"I'm serious, Sammy. We go back a long way. You don't need to play me. Is Miriam's story true? God knows there are enough real stories that you don't need to invent one."

"It's true. Harry, relax. Everything she said happened to her really happened. She doesn't know if Sandra is still alive. Those bastards use uncertainty as another weapon in their arsenal."

"So why the goddamn game?"

"What game, exactly?"

"I went to see Miriam this morning. There was a dark green Grenadier 1924 Special Edition parked outside. I waited five minutes, and Gordon came trotting out. It turns out that it was you and Gordon who approached Miriam, not the other way around, and you dispatched her to rope me into this job. You didn't need to do that, and you know it. So why did you? What stopped you from coming to me directly?"

He was quiet so long I thought he wasn't going to answer, but finally he took a deep breath and said, "Colonel Gordon vetoed it."

"What are you talking about?"

"Miriam is my sister."

"Son of a bitch! You never told me—"

"In our business you don't talk about the people who matter to you, do you?"

"No. I guess not."

"That was my nephew they decapitated and my niece they abducted. These are the things we live with day to day and try to remain civilized.'

"Sam, I'm sorry. But why didn't you tell me?"

"I told you, Colonel Gordon vetoed it. When the ceasefire was agreed on, we were in the process of planning an operation to go in and get all fifty hostages. The politicians said no. The Americans would negotiate their release."

He shrugged and took his hands off the wheel so he could spread them in a gesture of helpless incomprehension.

"Negotiate. It's like some punk comes up to you, puts a gun to your head, and tells you, let's negotiate about you giving me your wallet. It's stupid. We can walk in and take them home. But we have to negotiate."

"Stay on track, Sam. What's the deal with Miriam and Gordon?"

"They were lovers, a long time ago. He was committed—I mean really committed—to his career, and she was looking for more of a stay at home kind of guy. Joseph was all that. He was what we call a mensch. A solid guy. She adored him. What she never realized, because Miriam is kind of naïve when it come to men and sex and all that, was that Benjamin never stopped loving her. He's a good guy, he let her go without recrimination because he knew he was no good for her. But he never stopped loving her, and when the Kfar Aza massacre happened, it tore him up. He vowed he was going to go in, bring Sandra back, and punish those responsible. "

He stopped suddenly. After a moment, I supplied the missing words.

"And when it became feasible to do it, they agreed to a ceasefire."

He nodded laboriously. "They agreed to the ceasefire." Suddenly he stuck out his right hand, gesturing violently toward Syria, and his voice had became almost shrill. "Look! Look at Ahmad al Sharaa! All the newspapers call him a militant, or a member of al-Qaeda. He was a fucking terrorist who believed you should kill people for watching TV or playing songs at a wedding. Now he is president of Syria, and we all have to believe and trust him. So what the hell are we negotiating for? So that the man who cut off my twelve-year-old nephew's head with a kitchen knife can become president of Gaza? So that these *fucking* politicians can grow rich on Iranian oil?"

He smacked the wheel with the heel of his hand and looked away at the passing traffic.

"And Gordon feels the same way," I said.

"Every red-blooded Israeli feels the same way."

"But for Colonel Gordon, it was a little more personal."

"For both of us. For all three of us." He turned his head to look at me for a moment, then looked back at the road as we sped south. "I know you, man. I know all I had to do was pick up the phone, and that's what I told Benjamin. But he vetoed it. He said he didn't know you, and Israel's position was too vulnerable to run risks. He said Miriam should go and talk to you, and he would judge you by your reaction."

I couldn't blame him, and I said so. It all went a long way to explaining the colonel's behavior, and it had a strong ring of truth about it. Above all, I had known Sam a long time, and aside from being an honest guy, he was a crap actor. Yet his passion and his anger had both seemed genuine.

Shortly after that, we arrived at Nachal Chanun on the border and the defensive constructions around the Erez check point. He came off the road, raising big clouds of yellow dust behind him, and wound his way through ugly, semi-military buildings until he pulled up outside what looked like a prefab office with a big air-conditioning unit stuck on the wall like an ugly wart.

We didn't get out because the door opened as we pulled up and Colonel Gordon strode over. He opened the driver's door and told Sam, "You have admin to take care of. I'll drive."

Sam muttered, "Sir" and jumped down, and a few seconds later, we were taking off in a cloud of dust again, headed for the checkpoint. They waved us through, and suddenly we were in a world of devastation. It was Armageddon. Everywhere you looked, there were the burned-out, crumbling husks of buildings that had once been apartment blocks, homes, shops, cafés. All that was left of these lives was rubble.

I noticed the colonel had slowed. He didn't look at me, but I sensed he was aware of me. As I looked around, I could see patrols here and there moving through the devastation. Where there had been apartment blocks, now there were broad, open spaces among jagged crumbling walls with broken windows like blinded eyes. Where before there had been roads, now soldiers picked their way over shattered bricks, rubble, and the burned pieces of extinguished lives.

We passed a broken, twisted traffic light that leaned over a marked crossing bordered by the charred remains of cars. He spoke quietly.

"Are you going to lecture me about proportionate responses?"

"No."

"What is the proportionate response to actual, intended, wholesale genocide?" Now he looked at me. "There is a lot of talk about genocide these days, when what they actually mean is massacre. Genocide, Harry, is the intentional, deliberate extermination of an entire race of people. So what is the proportionate response to that?"

"I'm not arguing with you, Colonel."

He looked away and muttered, "They reaped the whirlwind."

We came eventually to the remains of a large intersection. Here he turned right, and we moved gently down a rubble-strewn street toward the sea. After a quarter of a mile or so, we came to an area that had been all but leveled, and at the center stood the crumbled, ruined remains of a mosque. Atop the heaps of concrete, twisted metal and shattered beams stood the bizarre, leaning dome, almost intact, except that the top had been lopped off like a breakfast egg.

"Khan Yunis Mosque," he said. "They still call to jihad from there. They still believe their god of hatred and slaughter will not abandon them. They do not realize he had abandoned them from the start. He was never with them."

"It doesn't mean much to me, Colonel. I'm an atheist."

He glanced at me, and there was real bitterness in his eyes. "Then you are probably closer to God than they are."

We passed a couple of blocks that looked like nothing so much as the broken teeth in a rotting skull and came at last to the damaged, scorched hulk of the Al Amal Hospital. Here he stopped the Grenadier and killed the engine.

"From here to the coast is no man's land. We could take them tonight and wipe them out for good. But we risk them killing all the hostages, and the politicians fear international condemnation." He shrugged. "Personally I figure we have survived several thousand years of international condemnation. I think we can cope with another six months. But the hostages —" He shook his head. "Let's do our best to bring them home as safely as we can."

"Where are they?"

He leaned his forearm on the steering wheel and pointed toward the brilliant, dark blue band of the sea.

"About a mile and a half that way. It's pretty much a straight line across fields and sparsely populated areas. You come eventually to a mosque. It is basically a big dome. They have, according to our intelligence, five girls held in the vaults under the mosque. We don't know what condition the girls are in, or indeed if they are still alive."

"But that was never the main mission, was it, Colonel?"

He didn't answer. He didn't react at all, except that his face seemed to close down, and a darkness seemed to cloud his eyes.

I said, "The main mission was always execution, wasn't it?" He still didn't answer. So I went on. "I've been there, Colonel. We all know the place. You get taken, especially by jihadists, and your chances of survival drop close to zero. And even if you survive, the damage they will have done to you physically and emotionally is such you can hardly call it survival at all. So rescue, though still a priority, becomes a secondary priority. The first priority becomes punishment—punishment so severe that they will think twice before ever doing it again. Punishment to ensure the safety of future generations."

"Sandra." It was one word. He said it to the windshield. "She was...*is*...like a daughter to me. Every cell of my body aches to have her home with her mother." He turned at last to look at me. "I don't expect you to understand. But for us, our children's future, our children's children's future, and their future generations, they are as important—*more important*—than our own lives. We have learned that we survive as a people. Bring her home, and I will be forever in your debt. I will love you as my own family. Execute those who took her, and all my people will be in your debt forever."

I nodded. There were no words to answer his. "Nuts and bolts," I said. "How do we do this?"

He climbed down from the cab. I swung down and followed him to the back of the vehicle. He reached in for a camouflage rucksack and handed it to me.

"Hardware. I'll tell you what it is in a moment." He pulled over a file and opened it. "This is a map of the area based on drone photographs. We are here."

He pointed to a spot on the map where the hospital had been highlighted, then pulled a red felt-tip pen from his pocket and marked out a path with small red dashes that led from the hospital down a dirt track and across fields to a crossroad.

"This is your simplest path to the mosque and should take you no more than forty or fifty minutes. Now we cannot be sure, but we believe there are access tunnels that lead to the mosque here in this farm"—he indicated a large hangar about three or four hundred yards east of the mosque—"and in the basement of this apartment block. It was bombed some time back, but there is still access to the basement."

He pointed to a partially collapsed building two hundred yards northeast of the mosque.

"It's a toss of the coin," he said. "We have not seen anyone enter or leave those access points for about two and a half months. Since we were informed that Sandra was to be moved there, in fact. Does that mean access is now exclusively through the mosque? Does it mean they have been locked in there and left to starve? We simply don't know."

He paused, shook his head, and sighed. "If you go to the ruined apartments or the farm and gain access, will you find guards in the tunnel? If so, how many? We simply do not know. And finally, if you get access to the vaults via the tunnels, will the vaults be empty, or will they be full of armed guards?"

"You simply don't know."

He nodded. "We don't know."

"Do you have a best guess?"

He tilted his head on one side and gave a small shrug.

"Like I said, we've been monitoring the access points we know about, and we haven't seen any traffic since May. That *suggests* the tunnel is not being used. Given a small amount of reconnaissance, my own feeling would be that the bombed apartment block is a better approach than the mosque or the farm. But obviously these are decisions that have to be taken on the ground."

"Right."

"Now I am guessing you may want to set some booby traps. So you have a little over forty pounds of C4 in your rucksack. I'm also guessing you'll need to make some silent kills, so you have a small crossbow that packs an eighty pound punch. It has a telescopic sight with night vision capability. You have a BUL SAS II with a suppressor. You also have an X95, a forty millimeter underbarrel grenade launcher." He gave a small sigh. "I know you guys like the Fairbairn and Sykes knife. I like it myself. I have also included the obvious detonators and night vision goggles."

As he had been talking, I had been inspecting the material. When he finished, I started packing the stuff back in the rucksack.

"This is the rucksack you prepared for yourself, isn't it?"

"Yes."

I zipped it up and looked him in the eye.

"What about the other part of the mission?"

He held my eye for a long moment. "I'll tell you about that now."

# TEN

I SET OFF AFTER DARK. GAZA GETS ELECTRICITY sporadically and erratically. As I walked along the cool dirt track under the stars, surrounded by the black shadows of the devastated, crumbling buildings, I couldn't help but remember Ismail Haniyeh's words after Hamas' attack on Israel on October 7th.

"Today, the enemy has had a political, military, intelligence, security, and moral defeat inflicted upon it, and we shall crown it with a crushing defeat that will expel it from our lands."

Ismail Haniyeh, the leader of Hamas' Political Bureau in Exile, was assassinated nine months later, along with his bodyguard, in Tehran. You couldn't help feeling he got caught up trying to make the facts fit the theory.

Colonel Gordon had told me I would not meet any patrols, and he was right. The streets—if you could still call them that —were dark, empty, and silent, and what few members of Hamas there were tended to remain hidden. They did not patrol. They stayed close to their hideouts.

Even so, once I had left the Israeli occupied area behind me, I made a point of sticking to the darker, shadowy areas and moving from one ruined building to another and pausing to listen at each stop. I heard nothing but the feral rustle of rats and cats and insects in the rubble and the dry grass.

After half a mile or so, the broken buildings fell away, and I found myself in an area of mixed wasteland and what looked like small holdings, fenced off, and growing basic crops. Now I moved from the small copses to small sheds and fences, sometimes crouch-running, sometimes crawling, always making sure that any movements or sounds I made were irregular and sporadic. Nothing ensures a lethal shot as much as quiet, rhythmic sound.

It took me a little over an hour to cover a mile, but finally, after crossing a broad patch of cool sand, mainly on my belly, I came to a farm with a large palm plantation and fields that had been recently harvested. Beyond them, about three hundred and fifty yards away, I could just make out, in the faint starlight, the domed mosque. To the right of that and about halfway between where I lay behind a dry stone wall and the mosque was a large, half collapsed apartment block. There was a rambling dirt track that led past the building, and I took it at a steady run. Thirty seconds later, I ducked into a half-crumbled archway that gave onto a large central patio that at one time had held a fountain and small gardens. Now it held scorched bricks and beams.

Colonel Gordon had told me where the access to the tunnel would be. I fitted my night vision goggles and entered that bizarre green and black world. I scanned the patio, and beyond the shattered fountain I could make out the black form of an arched doorway. I was about to move toward it when a green luminescence seemed to waver at its center. I froze.

It was a man. He stood in the doorway looking from left to right. In his green hands, he held the black form of an assault rifle. I had the crossbow hanging on the back of the rucksack. I removed it, cocked it, and fitted the bolt. I figured he was twenty feet away, maybe a little more. I removed the goggle, and he became invisible, but when I peered through the night scope, he was large as life and glowing. I pulled the trigger. He must have heard the slight clack and whisper because I saw his head turn.

Eighty pounds of pressure on a tiny, razor-sharp tip will drive a bolt right through a man. He stood very still for a moment. I saw him look down, like he was searching for something on his chest. Then he sank quietly to the ground.

I waited a full minute. Nothing happened, so I moved quietly to the shattered fountain. Nothing happened again, so I moved up to the dead body lying in the doorway. I lay on my belly and peered inside. Three stone steps led down to a closed door. Maybe he was alone. Maybe they were short-staffed. Or maybe there was a guy on the other side of the door raising the alarm and waiting to shoot me. If that was the case, the longer I waited, the worse the situation would get.

I put the X-95 to my shoulder, stepped down, and wrenched open the door. There was nothing there except darkness and more stairs going down. I followed them to a depth of maybe twenty-five or thirty feet. There I came to another door, which I opened with a swift movement and stood back. Nothing happened, so I eased my way in. The tunnel ran right and left. Even with the goggles, it was dark. There was practically zero light down there.

I wedged the door open so that we would be able to find it if we came back that way and to allow at least a little light for the goggles to work with. The bad news was that I could barely see a damned thing. The good news was that, even though they had a guard on the entrance, if it was this dark they were not using it—at least not on a regular basis.

I set off at a good, steady pace, but I had about two hundred yards to cover, which was a good ten minutes in those conditions. But after thirty or forty seconds, it had become so dark that not even the goggles could pick up any ambient light. Using a flashlight or my cell was like hanging a luminous target around my neck, but it was either take the risk or abort. In the end, I cut one of the webbing pockets from the rucksack and suspended my cell from the end of the X-95, five or six feet away to my right and ahead of me. A misleading target that would give me the chance to hit the deck and return fire.

As it was, twelve minutes later I had seen no one and, apparently, I had not been seen either. Ahead of me, a door emerged from the shadows on my left. This one was steel, painted blue, and looked very locked. I tried it, and it was as locked as it looked. My options were an ounce of C4 or a Swiss Army knife. The lock was anything but sophisticated, so I rammed in the small screwdriver, and after a few seconds, it swung open, revealing a dingy, concrete entrance with a bare bulb hanging from the ceiling. Ahead and to the left, a narrow staircase wound upward and out of sight, presumably to the vaults below the mosque.

I climbed the stairs, taking each step as though it was the last, with my back against the wall, the X-95 at my shoulder and my finger on the trigger. It was a spiral, and my visibility was never more than six or seven feet in front of me. If I encountered anyone, my reactions would have to be instantaneous.

After what seemed like an eternal cycle going nowhere,

eventually a high stone arch crept into view. Beyond it were three high domes lost in shadows. Very slowly and very quietly I lay down, keeping close to the inside of the spiral. What light there was was a limpid yellow provided by a couple of bare bulbs that hung from the high ceilings. It was a large area, maybe fifty or sixty feet across and supported by a forest of arches, the light was poor, and the visibility was very limited. The question was as Colonel Gordon had said. Had they left them here to starve to death? Or did they have them locked up under guard?

I remained motionless and listening for a minute or two and gradually began to pick up faint, rhythmic sounds. It was the repeated sound of a soft scrape, a soft thud, a muttered voice, and the process repeated again. There was something familiar about it. I crawled to the top of the stairs, peered, and tried to penetrate the shadows but saw nothing. Then I got to my feet in a crouch and made it to the nearest column.

Nobody shot me.

Now the sound was louder. I waited and decided I could hear four voices. Their utterances were brief and made in undertones. Then there was the quiet rustle. But suddenly I was startled by a loud shout.

"*Gašashta! Gašashta!*"

My belly burned. I raised the weapon and spun, looking for whoever had spotted me. But the next moment loud laughter echoed among the arches and the shadowed domes. And another voice cried out, "*Lam 'aghash! Lam 'aghash!*"

There was pounding on a wooden table and more laughter. I lay flat on the floor and eased myself around the column, keeping low in the shadows. Now I could see the far end of the vaults. There was a row of low arches, maybe five foot high, sealed off with metal grills. Inside, beyond the grills, I could just make out human figures. These were their inhuman cells.

Outside the cells there was a table, and seated around it were four men. One had lots of curly black hair and a beard and moustache you could probably film nature documentaries in. Opposite him was a clean-shaven guy in his twenties with short hair, jeans, and a military T-shirt. These two were shouting at each other and laughing. On this guy's right, with his back to me, was a guy with a big moustache who looked like the lovechild of Saddam Hussein and Pablo Escobar. Opposite him, and most likely to see me, was a kid who couldn't have been more than sixteen. His face said he was engaged in a jihad against zits and he was losing. He had an embarrassing moustache and a single eyebrow that would have made him proud as a moustache. On the table between them was a pack of cards. If you'd asked me, I would have told you Sharia law had to forbid cards. They have images of human beings, which is forbidden in Islam, they are used for gambling, which is also forbidden in Islam, and they distract you from thinking about how cool God is, which is a must in Islam.

But here these guys were, happily shuffling the deck, and nobody had cut their hands off. I guess it just goes to show that rules are what you make 'em.

I searched for and found four Fateh assault rifles. They were leaning, two against a wall and two against two separate columns. I couldn't see the safety, but two got you twenty it was in the on position.

So the next question was how to execute the kill. I couldn't spray them from where I was because the risk of hitting the people in the cells was too high. Even walking up and delivering controlled bursts presented a high risk for the girls—if that's who they were. So either I had to circle around or I had to draw them to me.

Another minute or so of scanning revealed the door up to the mosque itself. It was fat and arched and made of very dense wood. It stood about fifty feet to my right in deep shadow. Painfully slowly, I started inching toward it. The domed ceilings amplified every sound and bounced them around the walls. So crawling on my stomach was out of the question. On the other hand, creeping, which was much quieter, meant standing upright or at least crouching, which made me a highly visible target. But somehow I managed to get myself between the four guys playing cards and the big, fat door.

I got up close to one of the columns, fitted a bolt to the crossbow, and got down on one knee. My target was between thirty and forty feet away. Something in the back of my mind told me that killing a sixteen-year-old kid was wrong. That at that age he might change, he could learn, correct his ways in the world. I didn't flinch. As that voice spoke in my head, I pulled the trigger. I saw him frown and look up as the shaft drove through his forehead and wedged with the point sticking out the back of his head.

That kid, if I failed, would go and rape and kill those girls. Whatever possibility there was of his reform and redemption, he had to die there and then. That was the bottom line.

There was a full four seconds of stunned immobility as his three pals sat and stared at him. He still held the pack in his left hand, the right holding a single card where he had started dealing. His eyes were slightly crossed, and his jaw had sagged into an expression of astonishment. And from the center of his forehead protruded the feathered shaft. He leaned forward onto the table, and that was like a trigger that made the other three jump up and start screaming and shouting.

The one with the big hair and the hirsute jungle on his face was making himself useful by screaming, *"Allahu Akbar! Allahu Akbar!"* in a high, shrill voice. Saddam Escobar and the military T-shirt scrambled for their weapons, shouting things in Arabic. Vaguely I wondered what would be a useful thing to shout in a situation like that. Nothing occurred to me, but by then I had moved to the next column. Saddam Escobar had decided that his pals already knew God was great and he'd stopped shouting as he ran to the wall for his weapon. The bolt caught him between the shoulder blades and pinned him to the wall.

Then the air exploded with machinegun fire. It was panic driven, but no less dangerous for that. The risk of getting hit by a ricochet was high, and the noise of the exploding rifle in the confined, vaulted space, the smack of the slugs on the stone and the whine of the bouncing rounds was overwhelmingly disconcerting. I didn't hang around for it. I went down into the shadows and rolled to the next column, putting myself pretty much behind the shower of bullets.

The Fateh takes a standard STANAG magazine with thirty rounds and a rate of fire between six hundred and eight hundred rounds a minute. Which meant that in a little over two seconds, they had emptied their magazines.

Saddam Escobar was ten feet away. Three strides. I stepped out. He saw me and reached, fumbling, for his sidearm. That left his throat completely unguarded. The Fairbairn and Sykes came up in an arc from my hip and plunged deep into the side of his neck, severing his carotid and his jugular. I let go of the hilt and stepped behind him, pulling his PC-9 from his holster.

I let him drop. The military T-shirt was standing in front of me. His skin had gone pasty, his mouth was working, and there were tears in his eyes. He threw his empty rifle on the floor and raised his hands.

I said, "You speak English?"

He nodded, said "Ye" three times, and finally made it to "Yes."

I smiled. I said, "It's your lucky day." He returned the smile uncertainly, and I shot him in the knee.

# ELEVEN

GETTING SHOT IN THE KNEE IS EXTREMELY PAINFUL but also carries with it the distress of knowing that you've lost that leg. They might be able to partly fix it, but the very best you can hope for is a troublesome, painful limp for the rest of your life. More likely, if you receive the wound in combat, you're going to lose your lower leg. So it hurts, and it is also very depressing.

I went over and hunkered down beside him. He was weeping and holding his leg and saying please a lot.

I said, "What's your name?"

"Ahmed, please, I don't do—"

"I have no time for bullshit, Ahmed. You have one chance of getting out of here alive and maybe saving your leg. You need to be smart and do exactly what I tell you. The quicker you obey me, the sooner you get help. You understand me?"

He was nodding furiously. "Yes, yes, please."

"If you lie, I will find out, and I will shoot your other knee."

"I no lie. I tell you. I help you. Please."

"Where is Mohammed Abbasid?"

He cried out in pain and distress. I placed the muzzle of the gun on his good knee, and he let out a high-pitched scream, trying to put his hands between the gun and his knee.

"No! No! I tell! I tell you everything! No! Please!"

"Where?"

"End of this road! End of this road! End of this road!" He said it three times, real fast, like that might stop me shooting him. "In hospital. He has rooms in basement. This is safe place for them."

"How many of them are there?"

"Twelve. Twelve men. They are cousins, family, like brothers."

"You're being very helpful. You help me, I'll help you. Now I need to know. Have these girls been injured, tortured, or raped?"

"No, no, no." He held out his palms to me. "No injure, no torture, sometimes we lie with them."

I gave an ironic smile which I didn't feel. "See, Ahmed, that *is* torture. Now I said I was going to help you. And I am, because I am a man of my word. See, I am not religious, but the Buddhists have this idea that we all get born again. And the last thought you have before you die decides your next life."

His face had collapsed, and he was sobbing violently. I went on.

"You have spent your life causing pain and suffering, you have spent your life serving a god of cruelty, punishment, and evil. Now I am going to tell you something because I want you to take these words with you. Those girls in there are people, just like you. They are just vulnerable little girls. And you have caused them a lot of pain and suffering. This is your reward."

And I shot him in the head.

I stood and turned toward the cells. It was going to be a horrible thing for the girls to see, but no worse than what they had been subjected to already.

I searched the four bodies and found a bunch of keys on the guy with the abundant hair and the Jurassic beard. I moved toward the cells. I tried to ignore the sick twist in my gut. There were noises. As I drew closer, I began to recognize them. There was whimpering, echoing small and damp, close to the stone floor. There was sobbing, and mixed in with the sobbing an occasional repressed wailing, like somebody, a young girl, trying to control their panic.

I came to the first cell and looked through the bars. There was a girl lying on the floor, looking up at me. She had matted hair, and her clothes were soiled and filthy.

I said, "What's your name?"

She didn't answer right away. She stared at me. After a moment her whimpering stopped, and she said, "Daphne."

"Daphne, I have come to take you home. I am going to open your cell. I want you to come out and stay close to me so that I can protect you. OK?"

I unlocked the cell, and after a few seconds, she crawled out on her hands and knees. I held out my hand and helped her to her feet. In the other cells, girls were approaching the grills on their knees and looking out at us. The sporadic wailing had stopped, but I could still hear occasional convulsive sobbing.

I opened the next cell, and as I turned the key, I asked the girl, "What's your name?" She had wild red hair, freckles, and very blue eyes. She was trying hard not to sob.

"Sophia."

"OK, Sophia. I'm Harry. I am here to take you all home, but I am going to need your help. All of you. OK?" I pulled her to her feet. "I'm going to need you to look after each other and look out for each other. Can you do that?"

They both nodded, but it was Sophia who said, "Yes."

I moved to the next cell. This girl was blond with dark brown eyes. She was gripping the bars and staring at me fixedly. I said, "Hi, what's your name?"

She didn't answer. She stared past me at Sophia. I unlocked the door as Sophia said, "Tell him your name, baby."

"Naomi." Her voice was tight. Close to breaking. I pulled her to her feet and gently passed her to Sophia. I gave her a look she understood but didn't welcome. As I moved to the next cell, I spoke quietly and evenly.

"We haven't got a lot of time. So I am going to need you all to stay real cool and help me as much as you can. What's your name?"

This last I said to a dark girl with black hair and black eyes. She was quiet, but she was staring at me hard.

"Are you one of them?"

"My name is Harry, I am an American, and I was sent here by one of your mothers." As I unlocked the cell, I said, "And if you were awake five minutes ago, you know I am not one of them. Be logical, sweetheart. What's your name?"

I held out my hand, and she took it. I pulled her to her feet.

"Invent a false name if you want to. I just want to be able to call you something when we talk."

"Abigail."

I had come to the last cell. I didn't need to be told. Not only was she the last one, but she was the image of her mother. She was looking at me steadily.

"Hi, Sandra. I'm Harry. Your mother sent me to take you home."

"Mom?" She nodded, like she was answering her own question.

She moved across the floor. I opened the door to the cell and helped her out. I could see tears in her eyes, but she was holding it together.

"OK, girls, I need you to move across the room, keeping on this side of the columns and not looking back at the table. When you get to the arch and the stairs, I want you to wait for me, and listen real carefully. If you hear anything, you tell me right away. Got it?"

They said they had it. They all held hands and moved in a line across the crypt, skirting the columns and not looking back at the bodies that lay strewn on the floor. I moved fast to the door that led up to the mosque, dropped on one knee, and opened my rucksack. I took out two pounds of C4, mashed it into a large ball, and pressed it just above the lock. I took a mechanical detonator and connected that to the jamb.

From there I moved to the central column and packed eighteen pounds of C4 around the base, stabbed in a mechanical detonator, and connected that to the door too. Then I ran to where the girls were waiting.

"Let's go! We haven't got much time." I started moving fast down the spiral stairs. "Stay close and look out for each other!" I glanced back, and Sophia had fallen into the back with Sandra at the front, and all the girls had their hand on the girl in front's shoulders. I gave myself a private smile and kept going.

When we got to the bottom, the door was still open a few inches. I hustled the girls through, had a look at Jurassic Beard's keys and, after a few tries, found one that fit. I locked the door and snapped the key. Then, using the flashlight from my rucksack, we set off as fast as we could down the blackness of the tunnel. The girls kept up, always with Sandra taking point and Sophia at the back, making sure nobody strayed.

We made good progress, and pretty soon, we were able to see the faint glow ahead from the door I had wedged open. I held up my hand and put my finger to my lips. I killed the light on the phone and crept up the stone stairs through the darkness. As I approached the top, I slipped the night vision goggles over my eyes, and the door at the top of the steps became a luminous green oblong. The guard's body was still sprawled there. I lay in the doorway and scanned the area. There was nothing. I listened for a minute. There were just those feral sounds of the night.

I turned to move down and found Sandra crouching behind me. I whispered, "Go get the girls, bring them up."

That was when the blast hit us. Twenty pounds of C4 in a confined space like a crypt will make a devastating explosion. It shook the ground under us, and whoever had opened the door to that crypt would have been all but vaporized. The central columns would have been swept away, and the floor of the temple above would have imploded. We lay there, hunched into our shoulders as the detonation smacked and shook the air, and across the stretch of cold dry sand, in the starlight, we saw the dome slowly crumble in on itself.

On the plus side, nobody would be pursuing us along the tunnel. On the downside, there could well be an enraged search for us all over the unoccupied part of Gaza.

"Bring them up fast!" I snapped it at her, but she was already scrambling down, rasping at them, "*Come! Come! Fast! We have to move!*"

They were shaken, exhausted, and brutally traumatized, but they ran up the stairs, with Sandra taking point and Sophia keeping behind them like a damned mother hen. I fought down the emotion and led the way across the courtyard to the crumbled arch at the entrance.

Now I let Sandra take point, and I stayed on the right side of them, scanning the bomb-damaged buildings on our right. On our left was just wasteland, but to our right was a landscape rich with potential sites for ambush. As it was, with Sandra's encouragement, the girls broke into a stumbling run, and in fifteen minutes, we were in among the devastated buildings that formed the border between that part of Gaza that was occupied by Israel, and the last, anarchic areas held by Hamas.

As we moved along the rubble-strewn remains of what had once been a road, we were suddenly flooded by spotlights from in front of us. They were the headlamps of two Land Rovers with roof-mounted spots. A voice spoke out from a loud hailer, ordering us to stop.

"*Do not move. Drop your weapons. Put your hands on your heads.*"

I dropped the X-95 and put my hands on my head, but the girls all clung to each other and, unable to control themselves any longer, began to weep. I snapped at them, "Put your hands on your heads!" Then I raised my voice and shouted at the trucks.

"*They are Israeli girls! They were hostages! I am an American! I just brought them from the Dome Mosque! Give us a break!*"

Nothing happened for a moment. Then half a dozen soldiers appeared like weird, deformed black shadows twisting and dancing in the glow from the spotlights. Two of them grabbed me. The other four took the girls, and we were gently pushed toward the fierce glow. Then we were behind it and there were men in uniform closing in on us, pushing, pulling, and jostling us. Next thing I found to my surprise that my hand was being warmly shaken, and my back slapped. Some guy actually hugged me, and as the girls were directed one way, I was guided another toward a Grenadier that was sitting idling nearby. Colonel Gordon was leaning against the vehicle watching me approach.

He gave a smile that was respectful but not very humorous.

"I didn't expect to see you again."

"Yeah, that's what my mother said when she sent me shopping for the first time, aged eighteen months."

He didn't laugh. "I'd heard you were good, but I'll admit I was skeptical."

"The important thing is the girls are back. They go straight to their parents?"

"Of course."

"I have to finish the job now, but when I'm done, I'd like to see Miriam. Have you any objection to that?"

"Of course not." I held his eye a moment. His look told me nothing. He asked, "How much did you use on the explosion?"

"Twenty pounds."

"The hospital will have patients in it. Some of them will be Hamas, others will simply be patients."

"I hear you. I'm going after Mohammed Abbasid and his boys, nobody else."

He pushed off the side of the truck and opened the door. "Lunch is on me tomorrow. I'll see you at the Hilton."

"I'll be there."

I watched him drive away with the red rear lights fading into the gloom. All around me, I was aware of the roar of engines as one by one the trucks reversed, did three-point turns, and drove away after the colonel's Grenadier. The lights of the last truck faded, and silence settled with the darkness among the jagged, broken buildings and the cool sand.

I turned and headed back into the war zone, seeking the El Baheer Road and the Khan Yunis Hospital, where some of the few remaining leaders of the terrorist group, Hamas, had sought refuge behind the sick and the infirm and the outrage of the international community. An outrage rooted in a series of charters which, through a peculiar twist of interpretation, condemned the use of self-defense and protected the rights of those who sought to kill, rape, torture, and inflict ultimate genocide.

As I made my way in the dark, through the blasted wasteland in that valley of death, I allowed myself a grim smile. I was bringing these boys a new charter. I was bringing them the HCHR: Harry's Charter of Human Rights. Article One says that when you rape, murder, and torture you lose any rights you had when you were born. And pal, if you rape, murder, and torture children, you have a special place reserved for you in hell, and I am your express ride to that place.

# TWELVE

About three hundred yards from the hospital was the bombed shell of an apartment block. I lay down there among the rubble and focused my binoculars on the glow around the medical center. I could see a couple of guys with rifles standing on the door, and every couple of minutes or so, a red Toyota pickup would drive past, kicking up clouds of dust. From what I could make out, there were two guys in the cab and two riding in the bed. They seemed to be engaged in some kind of random search of the area. They never seemed to get much farther than the El Baheer Road, and their search seemed to be focused on an area stretching to maybe three hundred feet in any direction from the hospital.

That wasn't a search; it was a desperate protective strategy by a group who was real short of men. Joining Hamas wasn't a real attractive proposition for new recruits right then. And with divine protection like they were getting, who needed plagues?

I made my way at a crouching run across the wasteland to an abandoned gas station. From there, I made it to a small copse, through a leveled apartment block, and across some more wasteland until I came to some scrubland at the foot of some buildings that had not been destroyed and stood across from the hospital. I was now less than a hundred yards away. Lying flat behind the shrubs, I could clearly see the two guys on the door and the movement of people inside.

A direct, frontal assault on the door was out of the question. I would have to find another way in.

The next hundred yards was an agonizingly slow crawl across a wasteland of sand, dry grass, and grizzled shrubs. Crawling across an open space like that, even at night, it is essential not to set up any kind of noticeable rhythm. It has to be slow, arrhythmic, and frequently broken up with periods of motionlessness.

I finally made it to the corner of what had once been a road. I watched the red Toyota bounce and lurch past and sprinted across to the side of the hospital building. From there, I scrambled down a small slope, vaulted a wall, and found myself at the back of the hospital. I could see the dumpsters for the trash, some open doors that smelled and sounded like the kitchen, and a broad, concrete area with a couple of ambulances parked there that looked like the ER entrance. It was all very quiet.

I thought for a moment about just strolling through the kitchen. Just another terrorist in a hospital full of them. But in the end, my gut told me the risk was too high. In the Mediterranean, you never knew whose cousin you might get talking to at any given time. Best to remain invisible as long as possible. So I slipped across the kitchen door and ran silently to the ER entrance. I peered in. There was not a soul to be seen.

Maybe in a place that had been devastated as completely as Gaza had been, the place where you are least likely to see people is in the ER. They've all been there already, and now they are either languishing at home or dead.

I hoisted my rucksack over one shoulder and strode in like a guy who is coming back from somewhere where he's been doing something useful and important, and he knows exactly where he's going. A couple of doctors and nurses passed me, and I swear they didn't even see me. Perhaps I was the kind of guy it was best not to notice.

For the next five minutes, I wandered around trying to look purposeful. I passed a couple more doctors with deep bags under their eyes and a few more nurses with headscarves whose eyes said their homes were a distant memory. I ignored them, and they ignored me back.

I had no idea what I was looking for except that Colonel Gordon had confirmed my own thoughts: If Abbasid and his men were sheltered in this hospital, they would be underground. Deep in the basements. Eventually I found a couple of cargo elevators. I pressed the button and stood waiting. A young guy with a cage on wheels came. The thing was full of cartons of different supplies. He stared at me a while, and I snarled at him, "*Allahu Akbar!*"

He went pale and repeated, "*Allahu Akbar! Allahu Akbar!*"

The elevator thudded to a stop, and the doors rattled open. I stepped in, and he came in after me and stood nervously by the buttons. I gave him a look like he was making me mad by breathing. He swallowed hard and said, "*Hal turid altagiq alsuflia althaalithi?*" or something pretty much like that.

I scowled some more, and he pressed basement one and then basement three. I grunted, and he looked away. At minus one, he pushed his cart out in a hurry, and the doors closed. My brain was working fast, but it made sense: He knew the jihadists were on minus three. He assumed I was one of them, and he must have asked me if that was where I was going. When all I did was snarl, he pressed the button anyway, taking for granted both that I was going there and that I was an asshole.

The doors rattled open on minus three, and for a moment I had no idea what I was going to do next.

I stepped out into a broad, well-lit corridor. It was kind of surreal. There were mundane, prosaic things stacked here and there, like cases of detergent and bleach, boxes of diapers, Coke, and a cart full of dirty linen. I could hear voices talking. They were men. One had a deep, gravelly voice. Another two were lighter and higher. I stood and listened for a while. Those were the only voices I could hear, and they seemed to be engaged in an ongoing conversation that wasn't about to come to a conclusion. I walked quietly and followed the sound as I pulled the suppressed BUL from my hip.

There was a door standing ajar. I pushed it open, and the three of them looked up. That is the moment when you really need to break their morale and at the same time even the odds. I did that by shooting the nearest one through the eye. His brains sprayed out the side of his head all over his pal's face. The dead guy slid off his chair onto his ass on the floor. His pal staggered back, screeching and wiping at his face, which left the third guy looking alarmed and holding his hands in the air. To the guy with the dirty face I said, "You speak English?"

"No, no English…"

"Wrong answer."

I shot him through the forehead, and he went to join his friend where people with no brains go. I smiled at the last remaining guy. "Do *you* speak English?"

"I speak! I speak!"

"It's amazing how quickly a situation can change. Right? I am looking for Mohammed Abbasid. Where is Mohammed Abbasid?"

He shook his head as he drew breath. I didn't wait to hear what he was going to say. I smashed the pistol across his face. Shoved him hard on the forehead so he fell back on the floor, still in his chair. I knelt heavily on his solar plexus, put my left hand over his mouth, crushing his nose in the process, placed the BUL on his left kneecap, and pulled the trigger. It was just a *phut!* But his whole body jerked and quivered, and his throat went raw with the scream he tried to put through my hand. When he was done, I stood and closed the door.

He was sobbing and gasping. I put my knee on his solar plexus again and placed the BUL over his right kneecap. He was weeping and holding out two hands to me like he could stop me pulling the trigger like that. I shook my head.

"No. No, no. You tell me where Mohammed Abbasid is. Three, two, one—"

He was waving his hands like crazy. His eyes were bulging, and he was half screaming, "*I tell you! I tell you! I tell you!*"

"Tell me."

"Down!"

I narrowed my eyes. "What?"

"Down!" He jabbed his finger at the floor a few times. "Down."

"There is no down. I just came down in the elevator—"

"No, no, no! Stair! No lift, elevator. Stair! Here." He pointed to the door, gesturing to the left. "You go that way, end of passage, stairs go down."

I stood, went to the door, and looked out. It was like he said. There was a stairwell going down.

"You find doctor, please." He was weeping again. The pain

must have been excruciating. I went back to him and hunkered down. "How many children have you decapitated in the name of God?"

He stopped sobbing but stared at me with tears making his cheeks shiny.

"How many women have you raped? How many men have you killed? How much pain have you caused in the name of God? How much hatred have you generated in the name of God?"

He closed his eyes and whispered, "*Allahu Akbar.*"

He wasn't getting off that easy. "God is great?" I asked him. "Look around you. What kind of divine victory is this? I get to walk away, pal. You die."

I shot him in the head and made my way to the end of the corridor. The stairwell was on my right. The stairs were broad and covered in sage green vinyl. I took them three at a time and came to a set of fire doors at the bottom on the right. I found myself in a broad corridor. Ahead it ran into darkness. On my left, a second passage was brightly illuminated. I followed it, walking slowly and irregularly, listening with care. Slowly the sound of snoring came to me. That made me smile.

I followed the noise to a set of double doors and pushed very gently. Through the crack I saw mattresses scattered on the floor. A quick count told me there were twelve of them, each occupied by a sleeping man. A voice in my head told me it could not be that easy. The voice was right.

I pulled the X-95 from my shoulder, slipped in a grenade, and was about to pull the trigger when I heard an almighty scream. Wood splintered from the door, and plaster exploded from the walls and the ceiling. I fell back, staggering, pulled the trigger instinctively, and saw the grenade hit the doors and bounce out into the corridor, too close. I turned and ran.

I didn't make it to the intersection. I hurled myself on the floor and covered my head and my ears with my arms. The blast smacked the air and shook the floor and the walls. I felt the hot air rush over me, and with trembling legs and short of breath, I staggered to my feet, checking myself for burning.

Behind me, I could hear a lot of screaming. I turned and ran backward, letting off short bursts of fire. I could see two guys on the floor and lots of blood. The doors were flapping as the men inside tried to get out. I fired again. The wood spat and splintered. Somebody screamed. I ducked behind the corner and took a whole second to search for a place to make a stand. It was just a straight corridor leading into darkness. There were the double doors leading back up into the hospital, but I knew I was not leaving this place as long as Mohammed Abbasid was among the living.

Then, among the shadows, I caught the almost invisible patch of slightly darker darkness that told me there was another corridor there. I ran. I sprinted until I knew I was half hidden by the darkness of the unlit corridor. Turning and going down on one knee, I loaded a grenade, put the rifle to my shoulder, and waited.

They charged around the corner en mass a couple of seconds later. They hesitated at the door, unsure whether I had run up to the hospital. I laid their doubts to rest with a short burst followed by a grenade. It didn't do much damage. I might have winged somebody. But that hadn't been my purpose. My purpose had been to draw them after me, and as I turned and ran, they followed, screaming that God was great. I skidded around the corner as slugs bit into the plaster around me and ricocheted, whining over my head. I slipped another grenade in the launcher as I ran. I was making it up as I went along, but ahead of me I could see a door. It was a fifty-fifty chance. It would be a death trap or a way out. I shot out the lock and kicked in the door as they came around the corner. I looked in and saw it was a death trap. It was small, and there was no way out. And now there were ten guns descending on me, just thirty or forty yards away.

I launched the grenade, let off two bursts, and sprinted for the end of the corridor. Behind me, I could hear panic and confusion. Another door loomed close to the corner. I covered my ears. The detonation sent shockwaves through the air and shook the floor. I shot out the lock and looked behind me as I kicked in the door. Two more guys lay in a horrible mess on the floor. That left eight or ten regrouping at the end of the passage. and I knew I had no chance. I was going to die. But somehow I had to take Mohammed Abbasid with me.

I stepped into the room because I had seen there was a second door in the far wall that presumably gave onto the transverse passage. I slung my rucksack on the desk and worked fast. I stabbed a detonator into one of the remaining packs of C4, slung the rucksack under the desk, moved it to a weird angle, screamed like I was panicking, and sprayed the door with fire.

Then I stepped out to the transverse passage and eased my way to the corner. I heard them arrive. I heard at least two, maybe three rifles spray the door with random fire. Then I heard the door get kicked in, and they all piled inside, scream-ing. By this time I had my cell in my hand. I stepped away from the corner and dialed 9.

The walls seemed to bulge and expand. Plaster and dust erupted from the walls and ceiling. The sound of the explosion was muffled, but the shock wave ripped the doors off, ripped through the air, and threw me against the wall.

I staggered to the corner and saw three men who had not

made it into the office. One was on his hands and knees, a second was leaning against the wall with his hands over his ears, and the third was sitting on his ass, gaping and keening. I knew I had to shoot them, but it was hard to get the BUL or the X-95 and take aim because the whole damned hospital kept spinning from right to left.

Then the guy who was sitting and keening saw me. His face twisted into hatred and rage, and he screamed and clawed his way to his feet and charged me.

# THIRTEEN

IT WAS A FRACTION OF A SECOND. I SAW THE BLADE flash from his belt into his hand. It was huge, viciously curved on one side and serrated on the other. I knew it was coming at me underhand, but all I could see was this guy's ugly, snarling, hairy face. I sidestepped and grabbed his sleeve. We both stumbled and fell to the floor. He was big and heavy, and he was sitting on my chest, twisting the blade around to cut at my hand so I'd let go. If I'd taken his wrist, he would have slashed my fingers to pieces. Because I had taken his sleeve, my hand was just out of reach.

But now he took the knife in both hands, and I knew I was going to get badly cut. Without thinking, I hammered my right fist into his balls. Lying on your back with two hundred and fifty pounds sitting on your chest makes it hard to get much power behind a punch, but panic can sometimes make up the difference. He cried out and tried to block my punches with his left hand while with his right he tried to cut at my face and my arm. I knew it was a matter of seconds before he made it.

Then it got worse.

I heard the two other guys get to their feet and stagger over. One of them hunkered down by my face. His face was twisted with hatred and plain evil. The other started trying to pull my boot off. For some reason—maybe because I couldn't think what he was going to do to my feet—that stirred my panic to deeper levels. I ripped my foot away from him and started trashing and arching my body, trying to throw the big guy off and get to my feet. He and the other guy by my face had started laughing and were grabbing at my face with their hands, trying to pry my eyes open. I knew I was going to die, and I knew it was going to be a nightmare death.

In my thrashing, pulling my foot away from the third guy, I felt the heel of my boot with my right hand. I screwed up my face, screamed like a demented daemon, and curled forward. Suddenly the ridged, metal handle of the Fairbairn and Sykes was in my hand, and I drove it with the savage strength that exists on the border of death deep into the big guy's ass.

He screamed a high-pitched scream like a woman, and I hurled him into his grinning, manic pal, wrenching and slicing with the knife as he fell. The grinning, manic pal reached for me. The big guy was half on top of him with his leg twitching and kicking of its own accord. In an automatic reflex, I rammed the blade straight into the manic one's throat, then slashed right, and blood fountained over the big guy's head and face.

My mind was struggling against a hot rage as I scrambled to my feet. The one who'd tried to take my boot was crouching, reaching for a Tondar MPT9 on the floor. I stepped across the prone, twitching one, grabbed the boot guy by his hair, and dragged him to his feet. His eyes were wild, and I could see he had the rifle in his hand. I didn't give a damn. I rammed the fighting knife deep into his solar plexus and levered the blade up into his lungs. Then I pulled it out and, as he began to suffocate, I spun him around, rammed the bade deep into the side of his neck, and punched forward.

I let him drop forward and snarled at his dying body, "What were you going to do to my *foot*, you son of a bitch?"

I hunkered down beside the big guy, who was shaking badly and bleeding out fast.

"You get one chance to live, one chance to come out of this alive and start over. What is your name?"

I knew what he was going to say because I had seen the photographs, and it made perfect sense that he would be the last to go into a closed room where there was a hostile with a machine gun. All I wanted was the confirmation.

"Mohammed."

"Mohammed Abbasid? That's you?"

"Yes, yes." He clawed at my shirt. "I can help you. I have much information. I can get money. Please, get me a doctor..."

"Confirm you are Mohammed Abbasid. You were at the massacre at Kfar Aza."

"Yes, yes, I can give much intelligence..."

"Wrong answer, pal."

It was brutal. I confess I had to search deep and find depths of brutality in myself I had never descended to before, but I took off his living head, as he had done to young David, aged twelve. I placed it on his chest and photographed it from several angles. Then I spoke aloud and told myself, and Miriam, "Mission accomplished."

I left the way I had come in, through the ER. I figured the state I was in, badly bruised and cut and drenched from head to foot in blood, I would not stand out much in the ER.

On the way back, I made no effort to conceal myself. I was too tired and too mad to give a damn. It took me a little less than an hour to get back to where I had handed over the girls to Colonel Gordon. The area was desolate and dark, and I was just thinking it would be too much of an irony, after everything I had just been through, to get shot by an IDF soldier. I reached for my phone, and a pair of headlights came on across the rubble-strewn square. I heard a truck door open.

"Again, I didn't think you'd make it, but I know your reputation, and I just had to sit it out and see. You look like you need a drink." I began to walk toward the headlights, and Gordon's distorted silhouette began to come into view. "Is that blood yours?"

I shook my head. "It was Mohammed Abbasid's."

I held out the phone and showed him the photographs. He flicked through them. "You made quite a mess," he said. "The other two guys on the floor were his lieutenants. Is that a blasted door?"

"Yeah, on the other side are the amalgamated remains of about fifteen men and a rucksack."

"That's over twenty men in one night's work. I've known air raids deliver less casualties."

"It's not something I'm proud of. But I'm glad the girls are back with their families."

"Come on, let's get you to a shower and a rest."

"Hamas will blame this on you."

He smiled without much humor. "Evidence, let alone proof, will be hard to come by. You haven't left a single witness, as far as I can see. And we will categorically, and truthfully, assert that we had no operations active in Gaza at that time."

I moved to the passenger side of the truck and pulled open

the door. I paused before climbing in. "You engineered this. You and Cotton sent Miriam to draw me in."

"Yes."

"If you'd just asked me, I would have done it anyway."

"I know that now, Harry." He gave a small shrug. "But I wasn't sure then, despite what Sam told me. And in any case, it wasn't about you, or me, or Miriam. It was about those girls."

I nodded. "I hear you."

———

SOME SIX THOUSAND MILES AWAY, Colonel Jane Harrison was shown into Richard Cavendish's large study. He had the French doors open, and the smell of roses occasionally wafted in across his vast oak desk. He stood and came around with both hands held out and a smile on his face you could fry tempura in.

"Jane," he said. "How have you been? We've been worried about you."

She held out her hand, and he squeezed it with both of his. She said, "That's very considerate of you, sir. Do you have any news?"

He gestured toward the nest of chairs he had by the open French doors. "Please, Jane, make yourself comfortable. Can I offer you a drink? Coffee?"

She sat, perched on the edge of the chair. "No, thank you, sir. You said you had heard from the kidnappers?"

He sighed and sat opposite her. "Yes. I'm afraid it's not good."

"Did they say why they had contacted you instead of us?"

He watched her a moment, paused, and turned to look out at the roses that flanked the lawn. "Their tone has changed. When they spoke to you at first, their attitude was that we were friends and allies, and they were doing what they were doing out of desperation. This time they were more hostile."

"What did they say?"

"They said they were disappointed by your response. They knew how important the brigadier was to you, and how much weight he carried, yet you were dragging your heels and prevaricating. Meanwhile, the clock was ticking for Israel."

"But I don't understand why they contacted you, sir. You are known to be a friend of Iran."

"They said they trusted me to be impartial. They want me to talk to Iran, as a friend, and they want me to talk to the president and warn him of the consequences of delay."

"Did they give any clue at all as to where Buddy was being held?"

He shook his head. "None. I recorded the call. Maybe your specialists can get something from it. I couldn't. All he said was that we had forty-eight hours, and if some action wasn't taken against the Iranian nuclear facilities, the brigadier would be executed."

The colonel repressed the sharp intake of air. "Their demands...?"

"They haven't changed. They demand low-yield nuclear strikes against four sites where they claim nuclear fuel is being refined and bombs are being manufactured. At the very least, they want to see that we are doing *something*." He paused and leaned back in his chair. "I mean, Jane, if they are right, we have a very serious problem on our hands. Iran with a bomb is an existential threat to our closest ally. We and the British created that country. We owe them some protection."

"But nuclear strikes, sir? You were always in favor of Iran's nuclear program." She shook her head in ill-concealed confusion.

He echoed her shake of the head, but with him, it was dismissive. "In the first place, those sites are hidden away in thousands of square miles of desert and among mountain ranges. The collateral damage will be minimal. Believe me, the political fallout will be a lot worse than the nuclear fallout. As to my support for Iran, I was in favor of their program for peaceful purposes. I never supported their desire to make nuclear ICBMs." He leaned forward with his elbows on his knees. "Have you briefed the president personally?"

"Yes sir, but obviously I cannot discuss that with anybody."

"I know that, Jane. Remember, I was president once." He grinned like he'd said something funny and mischievous. "Without giving away anything that you shouldn't, and I really respect your integrity here, Jane, did you get the impression that he was inclined to nuke the Iranians?"

"I couldn't possibly answer that sir, even if I knew, which I don't. What transpires in a private briefing with the president is protected by the strictest security and is classified top secret. Especially in a matter like this."

He held up a hand. "Of course, Jane, and I do not want to put you on the spot. I was just thinking of the brigadier and what I could do to help him. He is an exceptional man, and I don't want to just walk away and leave him stranded."

"No, sir."

He laughed suddenly. "Well, I'm sure you know that I am not one of the president's favorite people, so it looks as though you, as the CIA officer involved, will have to brief the president again and take him the recording." He frowned and seemed to fumble his words for a moment. "Do you uh, have a man on the ground?"

She stared at him for a long moment, and finally asked, "Where, sir?"

"Oh!" His eyebrows rose and his jaw dropped slack. "No," he said, "I meant metaphorically. Like an officer in charge of the investigation, that sort of thing."

"Yes, sir, but not a man. I am in charge of the investigation. Sir, have you any reason to believe you might know where the brigadier is being held?"

"No, Jane. You know I'd tell you if I thought I knew. But..." He sighed and spread his hands. "It's just a stupid notion which must have crossed everybody's mind by now, that if he has been abducted by Israelis, surely they would have taken him to Israel!"

"That doesn't follow logically, sir, no."

"I mean, hear me out, Colonel. If they keep him in North America, they are going to have the FBI hunting them like dogs. If they take him to Europe, they are going to have the CIA cooperating with Europol and local law enforcement. Russia and China are out of the question, Africa and the South Pacific are too complicated. But Israel? They have deserts and mountains and probably plenty of unofficial support from both the Mossad and the IDF. It make sense to me. I'd put a man on the ground out there."

She repressed a sigh. "I'll put it to the director and also to the president, sir. Unless there is anything else of importance, I think I should get this information and the tape to the president. I am very grateful to you, sir, for having called me."

"Sure thing. I'll keep you posted, and I hope you'll keep me posted as far as you can."

"Of course, sir." She nodded and stood. He stood with her and took a flash drive from his pocket, handed it to her, then took her hand in both of his.

"You take good care of yourself, you hear?"

She disengaged herself and made quickly for the door.

In her car pulling out of the drive and heading back toward the city, she fought to control her emotions. She had been given a direct line to the president's private security advisor. She called him, and he answered on the first ring.

"Colonel, any news?"

"Yes, I have just been speaking to former president Cavendish. He has informed me that the brigadier's abductors have been in touch with him. He has provided me with a recording of the conversation, but in essence, as he has described it to me, they are disappointed with the president's response, and if action is not taken against Iran within forty-eight hours—that is, nuclear strikes on their nuclear facilities—they will execute the brigadier."

"Jesus Christ! They can't be serious."

"Sir, Mr. Cavendish said that he himself supported the demand. That strategic, low-yield bombs in those desert mountains would cause little collateral damage."

"You'd better get here and talk to the president." He hesitated a moment. "What's this guy got, Colonel? He's a low value British officer nobody's ever heard of. I don't even know what he's doing here. Why isn't he in the UK?"

For a moment, she was about to tell him she had no idea. Then it struck her that right then, the brigadier needed all the help he could get.

"He's got dirt on everybody, sir. And I do mean everybody. He probably has dirt on you, sir. And everybody is terrified that if they kill him, tomorrow morning they will all be reading about themselves in the *Washington Post*."

He was quiet for a long time. Finally he said, "Are you serious?"

"Yeah. He works in intelligence over here, joint cooperation programs, and he is highly respected in the very highest circles. Whoever took him must have known that."

"OK, I'd better let the president know you're on your way."

"I'll be there in a couple of hours."

She hung up, and her phone started ringing. The screen said *Harry Bauer*.

# FOURTEEN

EARLY THAT MORNING, TWO MEN ARRIVED AT BEN Gurion International Airport, twelve miles outside Tel Aviv. They arrived on different flights, one from Gatwick, outside London, the other from Manchester, in the United Kingdom.

The first to arrive handed over his passport and identified himself as Michael Coen, a British national. His reason for traveling to Israel was to make a pilgrimage to *HaKotel HaMa'aravi*, the Western Wall. He took a taxi to the Prozdor Restaurant on Mendel Mokher Sfarim Street, near Frishman Beach, and on the way engaged the driver in conversation about how, after generations living in England, he was now discovering his Jewish roots and was thinking about moving to Israel. The driver thought he was a pain in the ass but was polite enough to feign moderate interest.

Coen paid his driver and gave him a handsome tip. As he climbed down from the cab, the driver pointed at the restaurant.

"It don't open till noon."

"Yeah, I know. I'm meeting a friend on the beach. We'll have lunch here later."

The driver shrugged. "*Shalom!*"

"*Kol tuv!*"

When the cab had left, he made his way to the café Xoho on Ben Yehuda, a couple of minutes' walk up the road in the morning sunlight with the shops opening and the roller blinds rolling up. People greeted each other, wished each other good morning, drank coffee, and started the day in gentle sunlight. It made Michael Coen smile.

At that same moment, Adam Meier was disembarking at Ben Gurion International, having flown in from Manchester. His reason for visiting Israel was to trace his family. He collected his Chevy Trailblazer from the Hertz office and headed into Tel Aviv. He arrived at the Prozdor at ten minutes to nine, found a parking space outside the restaurant, and made his way up the hill to the Xoho. He was about to push inside but stopped and stared at the guy reading the *Spectator Magazine*. He had a cappuccino in front of him and a slice of carrot cake.

"Mike?"

Michael Coen looked up from the article. His eyebrows rose, and he laughed.

"Adam? What the hell!" He got up, and the two men embraced. "What the hell are you doing here?"

Adam laughed again and spread his hands. "What am I doing here? What the hell are *you* doing here?"

"Sit down, man, have breakfast with me. How long have you been here? I just arrived like half an hour ago."

"You gotta be shitting me, man! I arrived less than an hour ago. We must have just missed each other at the airport." He turned to the waitress who had arrived and gestured at

Michael. "One of my oldest friends. I had no idea he was here. Can you believe that? Listen, give me a double espresso and a smoked salmon bagel. Can you do that?"

She gave a nice smile. "I sure can. Happy meetings!"

She left, and he turned back to Michael. "So what are you doing here, Mike?"

"Ahhh..." He shook his head. "It's been growing on me for a few years. You know that. And the events in Gaza, Iran, now Syria. It just put a fucking great magnifying glass over it. "I'm Jewish, Ad'. We both are. Living in London, it's easy to forget that. So I came on a pilgrimage."

Adam's eyebrows shot up, and he leaned forward. "A *pilgrimage?* Seriously?"

"Yeah, seriously. I want to reconnect, man. This is the planet of lost souls, dude. I want to find my way back." They were quiet for a moment, then Michael asked, "What about you?"

He shook his head again. "Man, this is freaky. Talk about synchronicity. I came to trace my family roots. I've had this drive"—he paused, thinking, bunching up his lips and narrowing his eyes—"oh, I dunno, I guess since I moved to Manchester from London. I felt like I needed to reconnect with my roots. Is that weird or what?"

"How long are you here? I want to see Jerusalem, the Wailing Wall, Temple Mount..." He trailed off.

Adam nodded. "Yeah, the most important thing for me is to trace Saul Meier, that's my grandfather. He was here in May 1948, man. He settled in Yeruham a couple of years later, when that town was founded. So I guess it's a kind of pilgrimage too."

"Man, that is so cool. I had no idea. Yeruham, where is that?"

"South, in the desert. Like twenty miles south east of Be'er Sheva."

Michael gave a small shrug and began to laugh. "You with anyone?"

"Who? Who's going to join me on something like this? You would've, but you were in London!"

"I'm in Tel Aviv now, man! Listen, it's Highway 1 to Jerusalem. We do the pilgrimage. Then it's Highway 60 all the way to Be'er Sheva. From there we take Highway 40 to Yeruham. What's that, twenty or thirty miles?"

"Sounds good to me, man!"

The waitress arrived with his coffee and bagel. She smiled and told him to enjoy. As she walked away, he raised his cup to his friend. "Here's to coming home!"

"To coming home!"

They chatted over breakfast, engaged the waitress in a friendly conversation over the best way to reach Jerusalem and what to do once there, then made their way back down the hill toward the Prozdor restaurant. As they approached the intersection with Mendel Mokher Sfarim Street, where the restaurant was located, they fell silent. Adam pressed his fob, and the car bleeped and flashed. Adam got behind the wheel, and Michael climbed in the passenger seat. They took off at a steady pace and took Bograshov Street east toward LaGuardia Interchange, where they would pick up Highway 1 toward Jerusalem.

Neither of them spoke.

It was a little less than an hour's drive to the outskirts of Jerusalem, but at French Hill, instead of entering Jerusalem, they turned onto Shaufat and from there joined Highway 60 going south toward Bethlehem, Hebron, and Be'er Sheva.

THE BRIGADIER HAD COMPLETED a thorough inspection of the house. The refrigerator was LG, the electric stove was Electrolux, and the washing machine and dishwasher were Bosch. These were all multinational brands and gave no clue to his location; however, the stickers giving almost invisible do-don't instructions and customer service numbers were all in Hebrew and gave Israeli numbers. The information on the stickers inside the fuse box was also in Hebrew, and close inspection in the bathroom showed that the appliances were made by the Hamat Group, which was pretty conclusive. He was in Israel.

It also revealed that the hinges on the doors and the windows were all inside the frames and could not be unscrewed, the glass in the windows was reinforced and, if he was going to get out of the house, he would have either to chisel his way through a wall or set fire to the house and hope for the best. Both were serious, feasible options, but the latter was high risk, not just because he might wind up incinerated, but also because it would attract attention from a very long way off.

But the chisel presented its own problems. Whoever had locked him in here had taken the trouble to remove any metal objects that might be used as tools, and the best he could come up with was the rack inside the oven and/or the screws holding the dining table and the freestanding wardrobes in the bedrooms together. He figured the oven rack and the small wardrobe would provide tools sufficient to get at the hinges on one of the windows, if not the front door.

So he climbed the stairs and went to town on the small wardrobe for an hour or so. It was satisfying, even enjoyable, to vent his anger and his frustration and remember some of the martial arts he had practiced as a younger man.

By the end of the hour, he had mustered sixteen two-inch screws and a couple of tough boards that used skillfully might chip away at plaster and, with a skillfully placed screw or two, might just eat through concrete.

"My plan, then," he told himself, speaking aloud, "is to chip away at the wall at the level of the hinges, with a view to digging out the hinges and removing the door." He stood from recovering the screws from the wreckage of the wardrobe, muttered, "Good show" to himself, and made his way downstairs.

It was slow, painstaking work. Stage one was to use the boards to chip away the plaster around the doorframes, in the areas where the hinges would be, by slamming the corners of the boards into the walls. Most buildings in Israel are made of concrete, and as the plaster crumbled and fell away, the brutal concrete was exposed underneath. Now with infinite patience, he went to stage two. This involved the use of a steel garlic crusher he had found in the kitchen, hammering a screw a quarter of an inch into the concrete, moving the screw up a quarter of an inch and repeating the operation, and then repeating it again until the concrete framing the door began to crumble. Again, this he did only in the approximate areas of the hinges.

Even with a decent hammer, it would have been slow, tedious work. With nothing better than a light garlic crusher, it took him close to two hours to find the first long screws buried in the wall, holding the hinges to the doorframe. Another hour's work had fully exposed the screws holding both hinges.

But that in itself was not enough. His hands hurt, his neck ached, and so did his back. But what he had to do now was draw the door back, out of the frame that was holding it, yet angling it in such a way as to force the latch out of the lock. This stage could be the hardest of all.

He went to the oven and removed the grill. With great difficulty, he managed to pry one of the steel bars free. He bent it into an L at one end and a J at the other end. His hands were now in extreme pain, and he went to the sink to bathe them in cold water. His plan, such as it was, was to slip the steel prong under the door and engage the L end as a hook. He would then attach his belt to the J end and pull with all his might. If he could budge the hinged side of the door just an inch or two, it would be enough.

It was as he was running through these thoughts while bathing his bruised, strained hands that he noticed the small cloud of dust on the horizon.

He dried his hands and ran up the stairs to look from the bedroom window. The car was perhaps a mile away, moving fast along the dirt track. If it was headed for the house, it would be there in two minutes at the most. He pushed out of the bedroom and scrambled down the stairs again. He pulled in the hook he had made for the door, put his belt back on, and stood with his back against the wall at the unhinged side of the door, holding the hook firmly in both hands.

One car meant maximum four opponents. Take three out before they know what's happened and you've evened the odds.

He heard the car pull up outside. The engine died. Doors slammed, and he heard two sets of footsteps approach the door. A key slipped into the lock, and at that moment the brigadier knew that there was a ninety percent chance that they were hostile: They owned his prison. So they were his captors.

Kill one, interrogate the other.

The lock turned. The door swung in a couple of inches, then leaned in as the hinges came away from the wall with a rending, tearing noise and crashed to the floor in a cloud of dust. The brigadier had known this was coming. There was no shock for him as there was for Michael Coen and Adam Meier. He stepped out as they stared at the door and swung the hook savagely. He did not aim for the head, where it would get stuck in bone. He aimed for the neck and savagely tore out Adam Meier's throat. Blood gushed and bubbled up out of his neck, and he fell gurgling and drowning in his own blood.

He could have taken Michael with the backhander on the way back, but he wanted him alive for interrogation. So he stormed at him and swung at the side of his neck with the blade of his hand. Coen weaved, stumbled back, and fell. As he scrambled and stumbled, trying to find his feet, the brigadier reached under Meier's coat and found a BUL M5. He pulled it and trained it on Coen as Coen ran for the arch that led to the bedrooms.

He ducked behind the wall, and his voice shook as he shouted, "I'm armed!"

The brigadier frowned.

"You're English."

There was no reply. He knelt beside Meier's body, keeping his weapon trained on the arch, and pulled the dead man's wallet and passport from his pocket.

"Adam Meier? What the hell is this? Do you know who I am?"

"Fuck you!"

"No, but as good an answer as any." He took a silent step closer and lowered the angle of his weapon. "Your friend was Jewish. Are you Jewish? Are you Mossad?"

He was close enough to hear the man's breathing. After a

moment, he swallowed and said, "Yeah, we're from Mossad. And you're in big trouble, man. You just killed a Mossad agent."

The brigadier smiled. "If you were an agent with the Mossad, three things would be different here. Adam Meier would be alive, I would be dead, and you would call that organization *the* Mossad."

He took another step closer, so there were now just two feet between him and the wall.

"The only person here who is in serious trouble is you, and the best thing you can do now, my friend, is drop your weapon, come out with your hands in the air, and have a little chat with me."

He did exactly what the brigadier had imagined he would do as he heard his voice getting closer. He swung out violently, holding his weapon out in front of him, aiming for the brigadier's chest. Only the brigadier wasn't there. He had side-stepped to his left and had his weapon trained exactly where he knew Coen's left leg would be. He squeezed the trigger and watched the plume of blood spray out of the far side of his thigh.

Coen screamed, dropped his weapon, and clutched at his thigh. The brigadier didn't think or hesitate. He stepped in, gripped Coen's throat, and kicked his feet from under him. He sprawled on his back, gasping with pain, and the brigadier dropped one knee onto his solar plexus and shoved the muzzle of the BUL where no man should ever have the muzzle of a BUL shoved.

"Now, old chap," he said. "Let's have a chat. Let's start with your name. Your *real* name."

# FIFTEEN

I AWOKE TO AN ABSOLUTE STILLNESS. THERE WAS A distorted oblong of light on the ceiling. Then I was aware that the sunlight reflecting off the pool was moving in waves across the oblong of light.

There was silence. A man's voice down the corridor, a door closing, some kids talking as they passed my door; but none of these things encroached on the silence. They moved around it, like water flowing around a still rock in a stream.

I closed my eyes and tried to hold on to the stillness and the silence, but they were gone, and I didn't know how to find them again.

Miriam. Sandra was home with Miriam. The other girls, Daphne, Sophia, Naomi, and Abigail. Did they have families to go to? I sat up with a hot, burning twist in my belly. The carnage of the room where I had detonated the C4 flooded my mind. Abbasid, what I had done to him while he wept and pleaded. I swung out of bed and made it to the bathroom before I threw up. I rinsed my mouth, showered with cold water, and poured myself a strong shot of Bushmills.

I looked at my watch. It was ten a.m. My conversation with Jane in the small hours started to come back to me. I called room service, ordered coffee, and started to dress.

By a quarter to eleven, I was pulling up outside her apartment block on the seafront. There was no Grenadier parked there that morning, but I sat and waited for ten minutes before climbing out of my car and entering the block. I was pretty sure I was being watched, but I still wasn't sure who was watching me. And I couldn't see them, which meant they were good.

I pushed through the glass doors into the lobby and rode the elevator to the twelfth floor. She opened the door as I was about to ring for the second time and stood staring up at me. Her eyes and lips were swollen, like she had a bad flu.

"Mr. Bauer."

"Harry."

She tried and failed to smile, gave a small nod, and said, "Harry."

"Is this a bad time?"

She shook her head. "No, please come in." She stood back. "Sandra is sleeping. The doctor gave her some pills. I haven't been able to sleep."

I stepped over the threshold, and she closed the door. I followed her into the broad living room, but instead of going to the sofa and chairs, she crossed to the big plate glass doors to the balcony and stood staring out at the ocean. I went and stood behind her.

"It seems I have been waiting an eternity for her to come home. Now you have brought her to me, and I realize it is just the beginning of the nightmare. What they have done to her, the pain she will carry inside for the rest of her life."

She gave her head a couple of slow shakes and turned to face me, searching my face for an answer that wasn't there.

"You went to hell to bring her back, but she brought hell back with her. What can I do? How can I help her now?"

"I don't know. I wish I knew."

"I sometimes think we will not go to hell when we die, Mr. Ba—" She stopped and gave a small sigh. "Harry. I sometimes think we are already in hell. And God has tasked us with learning how to get out."

"You may be right."

"Are you a religious man, Harry?"

"No."

"You are not a Jew?"

"No."

She smiled for the first time, but it had a trace of sadness in it. "And yet you did this for us."

"Miriam, I need to talk to you. I need to ask you some questions. I know this is a bad time, but time is a really important consideration right now. A close friend of mine could lose his life."

She frowned at me. "How can I help?"

She didn't wait for an answer. She pushed gently past me and went to sit on the sofa.

"How can *I* help with that?"

She didn't look at me as she asked. She was looking at her hands.

"You've known Colonel Gordon a long time, haven't you?"

She looked up at me now, and her eyes seemed to flit over my face. She turned back to her hands before answering.

"Yes. Years. Many years. I told you that before."

"You and he, and Sam Cotton, you discussed ways to get me to come and bring back the girls, your daughter."

She didn't say anything. I went and sat opposite her.

"I'm glad you did. I'm glad your daughter is back home with you."

"Thank you." It was barely a whisper. "I haven't thanked you."

"What else did Colonel Gordon and Sam discuss, Miriam?"

"I don't know. I didn't really listen."

"I get that. All you could think about was your daughter." She nodded. "But there was another part to the plan, wasn't there?"

I made it a statement, not a question, and she said, "I think so."

"Something to do with New York..."

"They talked about Long Island."

"Oyster Bay?"

"Yes." She raised her eyes to meet mine and nodded. "Oyster Bay, yes."

Can you remember what they said about Oyster Bay?"

"I'm sorry."

I felt like a real heel doing it, but I figured I had no choice. I said, "Miriam, last night I risked my life to save your daughter's. Now I am asking you to help me save my friend. He's a good man, and his life is in danger. If you have any information that could help me, I need to know."

She looked distressed. "I didn't pay much attention. I think they had a request from the United States to turn a blind eye and not get involved. A quid pro quo. An American group was bringing somebody, and they wanted us, Israel..."

She trailed off. I said, "To turn a blind eye?"

She shrugged. "Yes, I suppose so." She studied my face. "Is that your friend?"

"I think so. Did they say where he was going to be held?"

"I don't know, Harry. Why don't you ask Ben? Or Sam?"

She had told me enough, and she was in no condition for me to cross-examine her. She'd been through hell for nearly two years, and now that she had her daughter back, I was not going to make more hell for her. She was right. The people I needed to be talking to were Sam and Gordon, now that I knew for certain. I nodded.

"Sure, I'll do that. I hope you and Sandra find a way. Don't let those bastards rob you of your happiness."

I made my way down and stood leaning on the roof of my rented Genericmobile, looking out at the ocean. It was still and flat, and a slight mist hung over it. I had all the pieces, I told myself, and they all fit together perfectly. But when I fit them together, they didn't make any logical sense. Eventually I pulled my cell from my pocket and called Sam.

"Hey, dude. I didn't expect you to be out of bed for a week at least."

"Yeah, I'm done here. I need to get back to New York. I figured we could have a celebratory beer before I go. You free?"

"Sure. When's your flight?"

"This evening. You free now?"

He hesitated for a fraction of a second. "Yeah, sure. Man, after what you did last night, of course I'm free."

"Good. You want to call Gordon and ask him to join us?" This time, he hesitated a little longer. So I added, "He told me we'd have lunch today. Also, I feel I need to be debriefed. There's stuff he needs to know."

"Sure. That makes sense. I'll call him."

"Where do you want to meet?"

"Yeah, I haven't got that far. Why don't I pick you up, and meanwhile I'll be thinking about where we have lunch?"

"Sure. Sounds like a plan, pal. We'll meet you in half an hour at Democracy Square, outside the MoD."

"I'll be there."

I found them twenty-five minutes later on the corner of Eliezer Kaplan and Menachem Begin. I annoyed a lot of people by putting on my hazard lights and pulling over to the sidewalk for them to climb in, Cotton beside me in the front passenger seat and Colonel Gordon behind me in back.

I turned onto Highway 2 and started to accelerate south.

Cotton punched me on the shoulder. "Hey, man! You're looking good. After the night you had, I thought you'd be wrecked."

I didn't look at him, and I didn't laugh. "When I'm dead, I'll have plenty of time to look wrecked. Meantime there is too much to do."

He laughed again, and it sounded a little strained. "Same old Harry. So where are we going for lunch? You said you wanted to celebrate."

"Yeah, there's a place in Ashdod, Bavarian Beer and Food. You know it?"

I made it sound friendly, but I had hot coals of anger in my belly, and I was having to work hard to keep cool.

"Sure, I love that place."

At Shapira, I merged onto the Ayalon Highway and started to accelerate. Cotton fell silent, looking out of the window as the suburbs began to fall away, replaced by sand dunes and the sparkle of the perfect blue Mediterranean.

At the Mevo Ayalon Interchange, I merged onto Highway 4, and the needle started to creep up from a hundred and forty kilometers per hour to a hundred and sixty, a hundred and eighty, and a hundred and ninety.

Cotton spoke again, looking at the dial. "That's a hundred

and twenty MPH you're doing there, Harry. Guess you need that beer."

I smiled but didn't say anything, and pretty soon we passed the turnoff for Ashdod and I kept going. The colonel's voice came from behind me, quiet and cool.

"You missed your turning, Mr. Bauer."

"I know. I had a sudden desire to see the dunes and the sea. I'll turn around at Nitzan." I was quiet for a moment, then added, "Nitzan. Doesn't that mean something like hope, a new start?"

His voice came back, still calm and quiet. "It means bud. We associate it with spring and the potential for life."

"That's nice," I said with not much feeling as I slowed to take the exit.

We crossed the railway lines, and I followed the road down, past Nitzan and in among the sand dunes populated with shrubs and trees. Pretty soon we had lost sight of the town. We had a barrier on our left and a sidewalk on our right which was largely covered in sand. I slowed right down, slipped in first, and mounted the sidewalk.

I opened the door, and before I climbed out, I said, "Let's have a look at the ocean and talk about the metaphorical side of buds."

I went and leaned my ass against the hood. For a moment, nothing happened. Then the two doors opened. Cotton stood not far from me, staring down at his feet. Colonel Gordon took a few steps into the sand and stood with his back to me. I saw his shoulders rise, like he'd taken a breath and was going to start talking. I cut him short.

"I want you both to understand a couple of things. I think you saw last night that I am a very dangerous man, and it is not smart to bet against me. I want you both to understand that.

That must be clear to you. What is maybe not so clear is this: If something happens to Brigadier Byrd, if he is hurt, injured, or killed, I will come after you, and I will destroy each of you."

The colonel turned to face me with an arched eyebrow. "Take it easy, Mr. Bauer—"

"No." The answer seemed to stop him dead. "This is what I want to get across to you, Colonel. I will not take it easy. I know about your involvement in the brigadier's abduction. And I am setting the ground rules for the conversation we are about to have. You need to assimilate this fact and take it onboard. If the brigadier is hurt, injured, or killed, I will come after you, and I will destroy you. Now do you both understand that, or do I need to prove to you that I am serious?"

The colonel came up and stood close in front of me, no more than a foot away.

"Are you threatening us, Mr. Bauer?"

"Yes. Let me be clear. I will tear your guts out with my bare hands and hang you from your long intestine. Now let me ask you for the second time. Do I need to prove that I am serious?"

"Colonel...?"

It was Cotton. Gordon glanced at him. Cotton gave his head a small shake. They were both able, battle-hardened men, but Cotton knew they didn't stand a chance. Colonel Gordon turned back to me.

"Drop the macho shit and the threats, Bauer. What gives you the idea we were involved—"

"Can it. Miriam told me she overheard your conversations. She didn't retain much, but she remembered enough. Oyster Bay was involved. That's where the brigadier was abducted. She also remembered you had a request from the United States not to get involved in some operation. They were bringing some-body over, and they wanted Israel to turn a blind eye. The expression 'a quid pro quo' was used. It doesn't tell me the extent of your involvement, but it tells me you know enough to make it advisable for you to turn a blind eye."

The colonel sighed and closed his eyes. "Harry..."

"Where is he?"

"You don't realize—"

"Don't explain it to me, Colonel. You'll just convince yourself you can get away with it, and you can't. I don't give a damn about your motives. I want one thing from you. I want to know where the brigadier is."

"Do you realize the people who are involved—?"

I reached out with my right hand and dragged Cotton a stumbling step closer to me. It took a fraction of a second. I twisted my left foot for leverage and rammed my left fist into his liver. A good blow to the liver is enough to make a hard man weep.

I didn't let him fall. I hooked my left forearm under his jaw, pulled the Fairbairn and Sykes from my boot, and pressed the tip against the side of his neck.

"Every second you spend spilling bullshit is a second the brigadier comes closer to death. How stupid do you think I am, Colonel? That mission you thought you sent me on last night was a mission no man could have survived, and a man with your experience would know that. You told me yourself, twice, you did not expect me to return. You were prepared to sacrifice me, Sandra, and those girls, as well as turn a blind eye to the abduction of the brigadier. You're some piece of work, Gordon. Now let me tell you what I am going to do. I am going to drive this blade through Sam's neck and cut his throat, then I am going to come for you, and I am going to gut you like a damned fish. In three, two—"

Cotton started to thrash, and Gordon's eyes went wide. He

held out both hands and shouted, "Bauer! Stop! Wait! I'll tell you!"

I squeezed hard with my left forearm so Cotton started to choke, and I bellowed at the colonel, "*Do I need to prove I am serious?*"

"*No! Stop! For crying out loud!*"

"Where is the brigadier, Gordon, in three, two—"

"In the southern desert! Near Havat Mashash. Just cool down. It is not as clear cut as you see it. Please." He still had his hands held out. "Put the knife away and relax."

"I'll relax when I know the brigadier is safe. Near Havat Mashash could be anywhere up to two or three hundred square miles."

"I will tell you. I will help you. Just don't kill anyone."

"Don't make me." I gave Cotton a shove, and he fell on his hands and knees, then rolled into the fetal position, clutching his belly. A blow to the liver really hurts. Anyone who's ever seen Micky Ward at work knows that. "The clock is ticking, Colonel. Start talking." I pointed at him. "If you were told to turn a blind eye, you were told where to turn it."

He took a deep breath. It was like he was trying to talk but the words were getting stuck in his throat. I put the knife in my boot and in the same movement I pulled the BUL from my waistband behind my back and cocked the hammer.

"Enough!" He closed his eyes and held up both hands again.

"Next time I shoot without warning."

"Five or five and a half miles south of the Ramat Hovav power station, traveling on Highway 40, it intersects with Route 224. Follow that route for a little over two miles and you come to a track on your right. At the end of the track there's a house. That's where he's being held. They are not hurting him. He's comfortable. I know because I asked them."

"That's real big of you. Now let's get something clear. You owe me big time, so I am going to trust you to keep your mouths shut. But make no mistake, Colonel, you set law enforcement on me, cause me trouble of any kind, and I will bring all hell down on your head. Are we clear?"

"You can stop threatening us, Harry. We are clear."

"When I get back, you and me, we are going to talk."

I got in the car, slammed the door, and turned around. I sped away. In my rearview, I could see the colonel watching. Cotton was still curled up in the sand.

# SIXTEEN

It was a bluff, but it was all I had. The fact was I had enough on Gordon and Cotton to disgrace them, end their careers, and put them away for a few years, but I hadn't been able to record the information or put it anywhere safe. If they put a sniper on me and took me, that would be the end of it. But they didn't know that, and I felt reasonably confident that they didn't have the stomach for a fight.

But that brought to mind a serious question as I turned onto Highway 4 and accelerated toward Kfar Silver. What had been Gordon's purpose in sending me after Sandra and the other girls? Not just sending me after them but setting up the whole elaborate plan with Sam Cotton and sending Miriam to meet me in New York, to tell me about her daughter. He wanted me to go and get the girls, but he did not expect me to succeed.

So what *had* been his intention? What had he wanted to achieve by sacrificing me and the girls?

At Ashkelon, I turned onto Highway 35 among vast, flat stretches of fields. I moved into the fast lane and hit the gas. It wasn't a Jaguar or a TVR, but I kept to a steady hundred MPH, and pretty soon I was slowing as I approached Kiryat Gat and the intersection with Highway 40, which would take me pretty much all the way to where the brigadier was prisoner, assuming he was still alive.

It was a forty mile drive to the intersection with Route 224, and I made it in twenty minutes, averaging a hundred and twenty on a practically empty road. I slowed as I approached the intersection, but even so, the tires shrieked as I took the bend.

The next two miles or so through the scorching desert took a little more than a minute, and I had to slam on the brakes when I saw the track loom up on my right. With the strong smell of burnt rubber in my nostrils, I rammed in reverse, backed up the vehicle, and turned onto the track.

There was no way I could avoid raising the cloud of dust behind me as I hurtled over the beaten earth. It trailed high and almost motionless on the hot air, like a big, amorphous sign saying, *Here's Harry!*

I saw the house pretty soon, and as I drew closer, I noticed the door was open. Then, as I pulled up outside and killed the engine, I realized the door was not open; it was just not there at all.

There were all sorts of smart, grounded, common-sense procedures I should have followed to make sure I wasn't walking into a trap where I was likely to get shot. After all, I had almost killed Cotton and sorely abused Colonel Gordon. Either one of them could have gotten on the phone to whoever had the brigadier and alerted them I was coming. But just as I'd had no time to interrogate Cotton and Gordon as I should have, I had no time now to take precautions. I had to respond, and respond right then.

I took the BUL from my belt, slid out of the car, and ran up the steps onto the porch. I stopped at the door with my weapon held out in front of me and studied the wreckage on the floor. There was the door lying among plaster and cement dust, and then there was the man with his throat torn out and a look of utter shock in his bulging eyes. And then there were the flies, buzzing and swarming all over his wound and his face.

I stepped inside and saw the second body. He was over by an arch that led to the back of the house. He'd been shot in the thigh and in the knee. He had bled a lot before he'd been shot in the head.

I went back out onto the porch and looked down at the dirt and the dust. There were the tracks. By the size of them, I figured it was an SUV or a truck. Maybe a Range Rover or a Jeep. So the two guys had arrived intending to do something. Interrogate him? Move him to a safer location? Or perhaps, as Cavendish had suggested, to kill him.

I turned and looked at the gaping hole where the door should have been. "And did what?" I asked myself. There was no sign of a blast, no burning, no scorching. Neither of the two guys looked like the kind of guy who could knock a door off its hinges, and in any case, there was no dent, no split wood, no damage to the door at all.

I stepped inside again, looked at the doorframe, and burst out laughing. I had a sudden flash of Sergeant Bradley, all those years ago in the desert, telling me, "You are never out of options, lad. You're only out of imagination."

Brigadier Alexander 'Buddy' Byrd was out of neither options nor imagination. But where had he gone? And how would I find out? I looked down at the two devastated corpses. "Dead men don't talk."

Not much, anyhow. I checked each of their jackets. Each

had a British passport and a holster, though the weapons were missing. He must have ripped out the first guy's throat, taken his gun, interrogated the second guy, and then killed him. The fact that they came armed, and the fact that he'd decided to kill the second guy told me he knew they had come to execute him.

I had a look at the passports. The names, Adam Meier and Michael Coen, were distinctly Jewish.

So how did that help? It didn't much, except that it seemed to confirm what Cavendish had said.

I rubbed my chin, feeling my brain reaching for something but unsure what it was. Knowing there was a contract out on him, he could go to the British Embassy, but if he'd seen these guys' passports, maybe not. On the other hand, with the contacts he had in the States, he could go to the American Embassy. But the fact that he had been targeted, and targeted right outside Cavendish's house when practically nobody knew he was going there meant the contract had come from somebody close to him, and that made either embassy option high risk.

No. I had to think what *I* would do. Because the brigadier would do the same. He'd go hunting for whoever had issued the contract.

I went into the kitchen and found some plastic bags in one of the drawers. I collected samples of their blood and also made impressions of their fingerprints. Then I drove away, back toward Tel Aviv. On the way, I called the colonel.

"Harry."

"Jane. I'm going to avoid buzz words, because there is too much we don't know it could be family. You following me?"

"Yes."

"So I found a nice house in the desert. It was real comfortable. It looked as though somebody had made a home of the place quite recently."

I gave her a moment, and she asked, "Did you get to see that person?"

"No, they were gone. But he'd left a couple of visitors behind."

"A couple of visitors? Were you able to talk to them?"

"No. Our friend had made that impossible. As you can imagine."

"Yes."

"But I got some presents for you and the guys in the back room."

"Like what?"

"Well, I got you two lots of deoxyribonucleic acid and some lovely prints. They are not Pissaros, but they are nice prints."

"You are a strange man, Harry Bauer."

"What can I say—"

"I know, the midwife told your mother that same thing."

"Yup. Send me the Company plane, will you? I'll send you the gifts."

"No. That will take too long. I'll send you the address of a place we use out there sometimes. Take the samples there and tell them you are delivering on my behalf—use my name, Harry—and the company I work for officially. You understand?"

"Yes, I understand, Jane."

"They'll fast track it and email me the results. I'll get them to you as soon as I have them."

"Good. The main problem I have is that I am trying to contact Al, but I have no idea where he is."

"He's a hard man to reach when he doesn't want to be found."

"You got that right."

"OK, I'll call this place and send you the address. Take care of yourself."

She hung up.

The address she sent me a minute later was in Jerusalem, just off Derech Balfour, near the University Library. The most direct route to Jerusalem from Yeruham to Jerusalem in a sane world would be along Highway 60. But it's actually faster and easier to avoid the West Bank, take Highway 6, and circle around north of Bet Shemesh to enter Jerusalem through the national parks, Haft Square, Sderot Wolfson, and finally enter the area of the Givat Ram Campus of the Hebrew University, along Derech Balfour.

I left the car in the parking lot and took my plastic grocery bag inside. The girl at the reception desk smiled at me like she wanted to look like she meant it but didn't.

"I have a delivery on behalf of Colonel Jane Harris, of the Central Intelligence Agency."

I didn't get any further. She pressed a button on her desk and spoke into her headset. "Dr. del Rio? The client you were expecting is here... OK." She looked up at me and gave me the smile again. "She'll be right out, sir, if you'd like to take a seat."

I didn't feel like I needed to thank her, so I went and sat in a vinyl armchair that squeaked when I lowered myself into it. I was just reaching for a *National Geographic* edition from November 1997 when a door burst open on my right and an efficient woman in a white lab coat, beige trousers, and beige hair that had not so much been coiffed as amputated, came striding into the lobby on legs that were too short to be strode on.

I watched her snap words at the receptionist, who gestured at me, and the woman, who was obviously Dr. del Rio, advanced on me with a smile that said time spent on good manners was time wasted. She held out a hand as I stood.

"You are Mr. Bauer?"

"I am."

"Dr. del Rio. You have the samples?"

"I have."

"Come with me, please."

She turned and strode away. I went after her, taking one stride to every three of hers. At least it felt that way.

We burst in through the doors she had burst out of and followed along a corridor carpeted in beige. We then burst into a comparatively small lab. There were two lab assistants in there looking at things through lenses.

"Leave."

They didn't argue. They left.

"Show me your samples."

I took them out of the bag and laid them on the bench, explaining what they were but not how I had come by them.

"It is very important," I told her, "that we are able to find a match for the samples with one or more of our databases."

"I will use," she said, staring hard at the samples, "the Integrated Microfluidic System for Rapid Forensic DNA Analysis. I need between two and four hours."

My eyebrows reached for the back of my head. "Between two and four hours? You can do it that fast?"

She frowned at me and narrowed her eyes like she was analyzing the skin on my face.

"Why do you ask? I have just said that is how long I need. You need to hear it twice?"

"I thought it took days."

"Hopwood and Zenhausern built a chip, long time ago, that can copy and analyze DNA samples using specially devised chip. We use this for special friends with special urgent needs. Label your samples, then go have coffee in the canteen. I call you when ready."

I found my way down to the canteen and had lunch, a beer, and several coffees. Two hours crawled past on the clock on the wall, and then another forty-five minutes. After that, one of the lab assistants who had been peering at things in the lab poked his head in the door and signaled to me to follow him. I followed him back down the beige corridor and into the lab. There I found Dr. del Rio, a man in his late sixties in a suit, and a younger man in jeans and a T-shirt that looked about ready to burst under the pressure from his biceps and pectorals. He also had a leather jacket under which he made no effort to conceal his P226.

I nodded to them as the door closed behind me and smiled at del Rio. "I guess the results were interesting."

The man in the suit answered.

"You are Mr. Harry Bauer?"

"I don't know," I said. "That kind of depends on who you are."

"I am Abner Schwartz." He reached in his pocket and pulled out a leather wallet. It told me he was an officer with the Mossad and held the rank of major in the IDF. "This is Lieutenant Daniel Almog."

Daniel Almog showed me his ID. He was also an officer with the Mossad and was a lieutenant with the IDF.

"I guess I am Harry Bauer, then. How can I help you gentlemen?"

"You are an officer with Central Intelligence?"

"No."

"But Colonel Harris, who is an officer with the CIA, requested these tests."

"That's correct, Colonel Schwartz. I am assisting her, but I am not with the CIA."

He nodded like that all made sense. "I need to know, Mr. Bauer, where you acquired these samples."

I thought about it but could see no reason not to tell him.

"Five and a half miles south of the Ramat Hovav power station, on Highway 40, there's an intersection with Route 224. Two miles south of the intersection, you come to a track on your right. At the end of the track, there's a house. The door has been knocked to the floor, and there are the remains of two men. One has had his throat torn out. The other has been shot three times—once in the thigh, once in the knee, and once in the head."

"Did you kill them?"

"Unfortunately I didn't. I arrived too late."

Lieutenant Almog spoke for the first time in a surprisingly deep voice. "Do you know who did kill them?"

"No. They were dead when I arrived. But I have a pretty good idea who might have."

"What were you doing at the house, Mr. Bauer? What are you doing in Israel?"

"The answer to both your questions is I was looking for the man who probably killed these two characters."

"Who?"

"Brigadier Alexander 'Buddy' Byrd. He was abducted in New York a little less than a week ago. I had information that suggested he might be at that house. I went and found the door lying on the floor, one guy on the threshold with his throat torn out, and the other guy in the living room, shot to death."

Colonel Schwartz sighed like life just kept getting more

complicated and at this rate he was never going to make it home for dinner.

"I think you had better come with us, Mr. Bauer."

I nodded. "Sure." I found a stool by a bench, pulled it out, and sat on it. "But how about first you tell me what this is about, and you send our friend at Central Intelligence the results of those tests?"

The colonel rubbed his chin, then ran his fingers through his thinning, gray hair.

"Colonel Harris already has the results. The two men you found were Jahan Ghasemi and Mahdi Jamshidi. They are Iranians associated with Hamas."

# SEVENTEEN

It had taken a little over half an hour to get to the Giliot area. We had gone in their Range Rover with the promise that I would be brought back to get my car. They had led me through bomb-proof security where I had had to hand over my BUL SAS and my Fairbairn and Sykes, and we had wound up finally in a windowless office on what seemed to be a fifth floor, but it was hard to tell.

There wasn't much in the office: a couple of steel desks, some filing cabinets, some built-in melamine bookshelves, and a couple of blue-padded steel tubing chairs. I sat in one of them, and the colonel and the lieutenant sat behind the desks, which were roughly at right angles to each other. The colonel pulled out a few photographs and tossed them on the desk in front of me. "These are the men?"

I looked at them carefully and nodded. "Yeah, obviously they looked a bit different when I saw them, but that's them. They were carrying British passports in the names of Adam Meier and Michael Coen."

Lieutenant Daniel Almog grunted. "Britain," he said. "She

used to be a good ally, but she has become as much a proxy poodle as Hamas and Hezbollah!"

Colonel Schwartz closed his eyes and raised both hands. "Middle way, middle way. Enough with the extremes. Let us not confuse the politicians with the people. So they were posing as Jewish Britons. That might have been to gain easy access to Israel. But then we have to ask: What made them want to come to Israel? The answer is, apparently, to kill Brigadier Byrd. So then we must ask, what was Brigadier Byrd doing in a remote house in the southern desert of Israel? Would you like to answer that question, Mr. Bauer?"

I nodded. "Yes, actually, I would."

He leaned back, fished a packet of Noblesse cigarettes from his pocket, and lit up with an old, battered brass Zippo. He inhaled deeper than you'd think possible and blew a stream of smoke at the ceiling. When he was done, I said, "Brigadier Byrd was abducted less than a week ago in New York, just outside Former President Cavendish's house at Oyster Bay. He had been invited there for dinner, and very few people knew he would be there."

He held up two fingers of his left hand as he sucked on his cigarette again.

"One," he said. "Have you heard from his captors? And two, perhaps related, how did you know where to look for him?"

I smiled without much humor. "It gets complicated. First, yes, we've had two messages from his captors. They claim to be an Israeli group called the Guardians of Zion. Their demands are that the president order tactical, low-yield nuclear strikes on Iran's nuclear facilities, which were not fully destroyed by the strikes in June. They say those facilities are an existential threat to Israel and have to be destroyed."

He had raised one of his brows a while back. When I finished, he said, "The Guardians of Zion?" He turned his eyebrow on Lieutenant Almog. Almog shook his head. He turned back to me. "Presumably the president had a good laugh and told the British ambassador it was not their problem. Why would these Guardians of Zion take an English officer nobody has ever heard of as a bargaining chip?"

"It's one of the key questions. Brigadier Byrd is actually a very influential man. You'd be surprised at the weight he pulls. The president has had several meetings with senior intelligence and security officials. He hasn't dismissed the issue out of hand, but clearly the bottom line is he cannot authorize nuclear strikes."

"Not at this stage, anyhow." He said it to the ceiling rather than me. Then he frowned and directed his gaze at me again. "So in less than a week, you found out where he was?"

"I said it gets complicated. I was in Israel for another reason."

The lieutenant cut in. "What reason?"

"A woman had approached me in New York. Her daughter was abducted during the Hamas attacks in October '23. She and her family were living at the Kfar Aza kibbutz. Her husband and her son were killed. Her daughter was abducted. When the ceasefire came into effect, she feared it could be years before she got her daughter back. Perhaps never, and the thoughts of what might be happening to her during all this time was too much. So she asked me if I'd go and get her back."

"Why you?" There was contempt in his voice, and he added, "How much did you charge her? Did you do the job or just take the money?"

"You want me to answer those in any order, or you just want

to keep asking questions?" He didn't answer. He just kept showing me his contemptuous face. "Why me? I was recommended by an Israeli friend who knew me because we trained together when I was in the British SAS. He knew I had a problem with jihadists who hurt children, and he knew I'd take the job without charging her. Which was what I did. And to answer your question, yes. I did the job. The girl, and her four friends, were delivered to their parents in the early hours of this morning. Mohammed Abbasid decapitated her twelve-year-old son with a kitchen knife. A knife he had grabbed to defend his mother and sister. So when I found Mohammed Abbasid hiding in the basement of the hospital on El Baheer, I decapitated him with my Fairbairn and Sykes. I also killed all his friends—there were about twelve of them, perhaps a few more. It was hard to tell after twenty pounds of C4. You got any more stupid questions, Lieutenant?"

There was a heavy silence in the small office. Finally Colonel Schwartz said, "So that was you."

"Yeah, that was me."

"The woman was Miriam Benzaquen." I didn't say anything. He went on, "Your arsenal was presumably parachuted down by the CIA Special Activities Center." You could spread the sarcasm like jelly.

"You know it wasn't. It was provided to me by a colonel in the IDF who will remain nameless. His concern was the same as Miriam's. The same as any humane person watching the politicians at work. I admire Mr. Netanyahu as much as any soldier would, but politicians have to do politics, and when politicians do politics, people die, and sometimes those people are children. He wanted those kids out, and I was in the right place at the right time to do it."

He leaned forward with his elbows on the desk and the

cigarette between his fingers. There was an inch of ash on it. He was staring at it, but he didn't flick it off.

"You're talking about Colonel Benjamin Gordon."

"Correction, *you* are talking about Colonel Benjamin Gordon. I told you my man would remain nameless."

He studied my face a moment, then grunted, and the ash fell from his cigarette onto the desk.

"I am having trouble with the logic." He stared at me a long time. "The *logic*. Here we have a group of committed Israelis whose aim is to save Israel from the existential threat of Iran with a nuclear bomb. It's understandable. It's a fear we all live with. A military man, a man of action, sees the Americans and the Europeans demanding a ceasefire because it is politically expedient for them. The Americans drop their big, thirty thousand pound deep penetration bomb and demand a ceasefire in exchange. Only the big bomb doesn't do what it was supposed to do. The politicians have to talk, but what does our man of action do? He takes action. He thinks, *If I abduct a high value target, I can get them to go nuclear."*

He paused. I waited.

"So far," he went on, "the logic is sound. The guy must be smoking wacky cigarettes because that is never going to happen, but at least his reasoning follows a logical pattern."

He moved his two hands like he was holding a ball, across the desk in logical steps. Then he spread his hands and shook his head.

"Then it all goes wrong. You tell me this Brigadier Byrd is an influential man. I say bullshit. I say if he is influential, you and five other guys know it. But my Israeli colonel doesn't know it. And my Israeli colonel did not become a colonel in the IDF by being an asshole. So if he is going to abduct somebody, it's going to be the president's son or daughter, and he is going to keep it secret, and he is going to provide the president with intelligence that will justify a preemptive strike on Iran's nuclear facilities." He wagged a finger at me. "That is the first part of my problem with the logic. The second part is, *where the fuck did these two amateur Iranian hit men come from? What? Were they employed by our Guardian of Zion, Colonel Benjamin Gordon?*"

I nodded. "I agree. It has all the hallmarks of an amateur job. But I am as confused as you are. The things that stand out are the choice of Brigadier Byrd as a hostage, the decision to kill him when he was still of apparent value to them, the use of Iranians masquerading as Israelis, and..."—I paused and nodded a few times—"the attempt to frame it as an Israeli operation. The objective was never to persuade the president to nuke the plutonium refining plants. The objective was to stir up and increase public hostility toward Israel."

"And while they were at it..."

"While they were at it, take out the brigadier."

"That is more logical." He pointed at me. "So why were you brought here?"

"A quid pro quo. A colonel gets his daughter back, and in exchange, he turns a blind eye to a US black operation which is not sanctioned by the president or the White House."

The lieutenant frowned. "His daughter?"

"It's a guess, but a pretty safe one. He's been in love with Miriam for years. She was conflicted, but ultimately loyal, if not faithful, to her husband David."

The colonel shook his head. "What was to stop him, or Miriam, going to you off their own bat? He didn't need this quid pro quo arrangement."

I smiled. "I wish you could ask my head of operations that question. There were four seasoned Hamas operatives guarding the girls. Anyone going in to get them would have to eliminate those guards and bring the girls back to the occupied section of Gaza. The deal was that I would get the necessary weapons and explosives, and the IDF would turn a blind eye to my presence, if I then went to the hospital where Mohammed Abbasid was hiding out with about fifteen men and take them out. I don't mean to blow my own trumpet, Colonel Schwartz, but there are not many operatives out there who would be crazy enough to do that. There are even fewer who could pull it off. Colonel Gordon didn't know me, but Sam Cotton did. He advised Colonel Gordon to use me."

"You are suggesting whoever set this up used Cotton to get to Gordon."

"It's the only way it makes sense."

"Colonel Gordon told me that if it had been his daughter in there he would have gone in himself long ago. But it's not that easy. You need very specialized skills to do something like that, and you also need the backup. In my case, Colonel Gordon provided that backup. But he had no one to provide it for him."

"So you are telling me this was all about rescuing his daughter?"

I shook my head. "No, I think there was more to it than that. I think there is real, widespread concern among the military that Washington threw the biggest punch it was willing to throw, and it didn't connect. Tehran still has the capability to make a bomb that will take out Israel and badly damage all of her Sunni neighbors, leaving Iran as the dominant oil rich nation in the Middle East."

We sat staring at each other a moment. I spread my hands and added, "It has always been the Israeli position that if Iran is ever in a position to strike her with weapons of mass destruction, chemical, biological, or nuclear, Israel would strike preemptively. I think a lot of people in Israeli intelligence and the military are thinking that moment has come, and American politics are getting in the way of Israel's legitimate self-defense."

He sighed, looked at his crumpled pack of cigarettes, and grunted. "Which is your long-winded way of saying that Gordon wanted to save his daughter and his country by using the world's most prolific assassin." He gave a short, humorless laugh. "The Reaper of Zion, who is not even a Jew."

His eyes strayed past me to the lieutenant. "Michael Coen and Adam Meier, Mahdi Jamshidi and Jahan Ghasemi, arrived separately, and Ghasemi hired a car at the airport. I'm afraid we were a little slow to pick up on them. Their documents were of superb quality, and facial recognition only caught them after they had rented their car and left the airport. The car they rented was a Chevrolet Trailblazer from Hertz."

"It wasn't at the house. There were tire tracks, but the vehicle was gone."

"Yeah. After killing his captors, your brigadier took the car. We found it."

"Where?"

"He headed south toward Yeruham, then turned north and east toward Dimona. There he joined Highway 25, but just after El-Mahdi, his car came off the road. There was a steep bank there. The car overturned several times, caught fire, and exploded."

I felt the blood drain from my face and a hollow, sick pit form in my stomach.

"Did you find a body?"

"Yes. He was badly burned, but there were items: his Rolex, inscribed, his military ID, his wallet and credit cards. It was him, Mr. Bauer. I am sorry." He sighed deeply and fished another cigarette from his pack. "We are very grateful—it may not seem so, but we are very grateful to you for what you have done. But I think it is probably time for you to go home."

"You still have a hostile conspiracy on your hands aimed at discrediting you and damaging your relationship with the United States."

He produced a smile that had more sadness in it than humor. "We have been the subject of conspiracies to discredit us for two and a half thousand years, Mr. Bauer. Somehow we manage to survive. You have done more than enough. Go home while we are still grateful."

"Can I see the body?"

"Sure." He shrugged and tilted his head on one side. "Forgive me for being brutal, but you may as well look at a chunk of charcoal. If you were fond of him, I would not recommend it."

I sighed and got to my feet. He watched me a moment and said, "Go home, Mr. Bauer," and I was surprised to see both kindness and compassion in his expression.

# EIGHTEEN

I DIDN'T GO TO SEE THE BODY. I HAD NO DESIRE TO see my friend and mentor converted into a chunk of charcoal. I should have called the colonel—Jane—but I didn't do that either. Instead I drove to Be'er Sheeva and took Highway 25 down as far as El Mahdhi. I had to drive four miles past the crash site, as far as Dimona, before I could cross over to the northbound lanes. Then I had to drive back another four miles and pull off the highway a little before the town of El-Mahdhi. I noticed absently it was a section of the road where there were no barriers. The barrier started maybe a quarter of a mile after the place where he went off.

I left the car on the desert sand nine or ten feet from the blacktop and went to stand and look down the slope. The car had been removed, but I could see the blackened, charred earth.

He was a good driver; he had a cool head, and he didn't know how to panic. What had happened? Had there been a second team that caught up with him and forced him off the road? I knew he was armed. I would not have been anxious to try and force Buddy Byrd off the road in a car if he was armed.

There had been two assassins, Iranians, and he had taken them both, then used their car to get away. He had turned right toward Yeruham and Dimona instead of the obvious route, directly to Be'er Shiva and Tel Aviv. I could feel my mind reaching—both routes led to Be'er Shiva. The one he'd chosen went via Dimona.

Why—I corrected myself, trying to think like the brigadier. Avoid open questions. What was it about Dimona that would make him drive through it?

I smiled.

I went back north a quarter of a mile and found an access point back onto the southbound lanes, then cruised down to Dimona. I turned in over the railway tracks onto Sderot HaNassi and cruised slowly among the dilapidated apartment blocks and suburban houses that had once made up a pretty town. Somehow it reminded me of the more remote villages in Arizona or New Mexico, the ones near the border.

I had suspected it. Now I knew it. I knew why the brigadier had come here. I eventually found my way to a place called HaHadas Street. It was pretty desolate, with large areas of wasteland and ramshackle buildings with graffiti scrawled over the walls and doors. There were a couple of nice houses nearby, but they stood behind high walls with very visible security.

I was about to pull over and park when I noticed a blond woman with a generous body and a dress that was about an inch too short standing at the corner of the wasteland, where there was a short street. I accelerated slightly, and she watched me approach. As I lowered the window, she leaned in and smiled.

"*Ata mechafes mashu?*"

"Maybe, but ask me in English just in case."

She grinned, and I realized she was chewing gum. "Looking for something?"

"You know what? I am. I could use a good smoke and some nice conversation. Then maybe a party. You know where an American could find those three things around here? I heard Dimona was a place a guy could find that kind of thing."

"It depends," she said and started chewing the gum that was in her mouth.

"On what?"

"On how much you're prepared to pay, dumbo!" She laughed to show she meant no offense.

"Hey, I've had a rough day, and it shows, but believe me, money is no problem."

"Show me."

I laughed. "You're not shy, are you?"

She raised an eyebrow. "Are you kidding me?"

I pulled out my wallet and showed her my credit cards plus five hundred bucks in cash. She winked at me and walked to the back of the car. I smiled to myself as she took a picture of my license plate before coming back and climbing in the front passenger seat.

"What the hell was that?" I said, still laughing.

"I sent a Whatsapp to my friend. If I'm late home for dinner, they'll be looking for you."

"Man, what a buzz kill. I just want a smoke, a beer, and a talk, sweetheart. Maybe a party after."

"No problem, lover boy. You'll get what you want with a happy ending." She winked. "I'll see to that. Go to the end, turn right. End again, turn right. Then you gotta go all the way to the circus, make the circus, and come back to the parking lot. You got that?"

"No." I pulled away.

"It'll be worth it. You'll see."

"I hope so. You kind of brought me down with that photograph stunt."

"You got something to worry about? Right here." She pointed at the intersection.

"No, of course not."

"So don't worry. Right at the end."

I followed the road to the end and turned right into a broad avenue with a central reservation planted with flowers. The rest of the neighborhood was shabby, but it seemed lively and friendly.

"I'm not naïve," I said. "I know you probably have to deal with a lot of assholes."

"You got that right."

"But listen, I lost a friend yesterday, and I could do with cheering up. I'm paying," I said, trying to look tragic but brave, "and you look like a nice person. Maybe you could pretend to like me."

She laughed out loud, with her head thrown back and her hand on my shoulder. "You're cute," she said. "I don't have to pretend, lover boy. If I didn't like you, I'd tell you to go to hell." After a moment, a little more serious, she said, "What happened to your friend?"

I moved into the circle and spoke as I steered left. "He rented a car and came here, to Dimona. He was kind of crazy, but hell, I was fond of him. Tall English guy. On his way back to Tel Aviv, his car crashes on the highway and explodes. He was burned to death. It's left me feeling kind of weird. Right here?"

She nodded. She'd gone very quiet. She pointed to a space. "Park there. I'm going to get out of the car. I am going to walk to the pub in the corner there, and you had better be gone when I come out with my friends."

I put my elbow on the latch, and the four doors locked. In the same movement I pulled the BUL SAS from under my arm and laid it in my lap. "Not just yet, sweetheart. Tell me what you know."

"I don't know a goddamned thing."

I sighed. "I would find it hard to shoot a woman, but not impossible. We have other options, though. How about if I go in there, to the pub, and shoot all your friends? Alternatively, I give you a hundred bucks and you tell me what you know."

She stared, but I could see it was not obstinacy but insecurity and uncertainty. I pulled out my wallet, extracted a hundred bucks, and tossed it on her lap.

"He was driving a Chevy Trailblazer, true or false. Get it wrong and I take the money back."

"A guy showed up yesterday in a Chevy Trailblazer. He was some weird, stiff English guy."

"He was looking to buy drugs?"

"Yeah. This is a small town. You can get shit here. We're known for it, but there are only a couple of places."

"So he spoke to somebody and they told him where to go and get his shit."

"Yeah, they sent him to Shimon. He's like the main guy, but when his next client showed up, he was gone. His car was still there, his door was open, but he was gone, y'know? It's a small community here, and we all kinda look out for each other. Word spreads fast. Are you undercover? Do you know what happened to Shimon?"

I nodded and sighed. "Yeah. I know what happened to Shimon. I'm afraid he's dead."

Her face seemed to sag. "Oh, I'm gonna miss him." She looked up at my face. "Do you still want a smoke and a party?"

"No." I gave her another hundred. "You better go commiserate with your friends."

"OK."

She climbed out of the car and walked away, slouching slightly and counting her money.

I turned around and left the parking lot, wondering in my mind what the hell I should do next. I'd had the hunch back at the house in the desert, when I saw he had killed the two guys who'd come to execute him. He was going to do what I would do. Because we had the same approach to problems, and we had the same training. He had realized that the easiest thing for him was to be dead. So he had engineered his own death. He couldn't use either of his executioners because the ruse would be discovered too soon. He needed a body few would be looking for and, unless he was prepared to raid a morgue, that meant he had to make that body. The brigadier was not a murderer, and there was no way he would kill indiscriminately. So he did exactly what I would do. He headed for Dimona, which had a reputation as one of the few places in Israel where you could get drugs, he found a dealer, executed him, rolled the truck and the body off the side of the road, and set fire to it, leaving a couple of clues to suggest the body was his.

So where was he now? What was his objective, and what was his plan?

I had a hunch I knew, but there were details I needed to clear up in my mind.

I pulled back onto Highway 25 and headed north toward Tel Aviv, driving fast. On the way, I called the colonel. It rang twice, and she answered promptly.

"Harry!"

"Are you near a shopping mall?"

"Uh, yeah, I guess…"

"Go buy a burner and call me back."

I hung up, and fifteen minutes later, my phone rang.

"Harry. Do you have any news?"

"Yeah, but first, have you heard from anyone here other than me?"

"No."

"Good. Have you heard from Cavendish?"

"No."

"Good. You'll probably receive news from either the Israeli police or from Cavendish, or both, that the brigadier is dead. He's not. But he's gone to ground, and I am not sure yet where to look for him."

"How do you know this?"

"I found the place where they had him. They sent a couple of assassins. He killed them, took their car, and crashed it to make it look like he had been killed."

I heard a strange, slightly disturbing giggle and ignored it.

"Now I am not sure what he's going to do next, but I have a hunch he is going to go after Cavendish. The Israeli authorities still think the brigadier is dead, and I am happy to leave it that way. I think this was the plan all along. And I think he is going to use this to go after Cavendish."

"Cavendish?"

"Yeah. I want you to keep tabs on him, let me know immediately where he goes and what he does."

"Are you giving me orders, Harry?"

"Uh, I think so, yeah."

She sighed. "Right. I have a dozen burners. I'll use each one once. But, Harry? Our lines are secure."

"I don't know to what degree, Jane. Somebody very close

to you wants the brigadier dead and has manipulated us so that very nearly happened."

"You know who it is, don't you?"

"Yeah, and so do you."

"OK, let me know when you make contact with Buddy."

"Yeah. I'll keep you posted."

The afternoon was moving on, and the heat was getting intense in the desert. I was assuming he had stolen a car, but there was also a chance he had holed up somewhere out there in the dunes, among the rocks. I shook my head and spoke quietly to myself. I wouldn't take that option. It didn't lead anywhere good.

What would I do?

I'd take advantage of the fact that I was dead. Then I'd go in search of my prey. But how? This was a case where the prey was going to have to come to the hunter.

Unless.

Unless it was one of those cases where the hunter waited for the prey by the river. Yes. I smiled to myself. Yes, that was what I would do, and it was what the brigadier was doing. But, I thought, at risk of taxing the metaphor to death, what was the water? What was it that was going to draw the prey to the brigadier? Because *that* was where I would find him.

Muscle memory took me back to the hotel. I had a shower and fixed myself a martini. Neither of which did anything to jog my mind out of paralysis. I went and stood on my terrace and looked out at the vast sweep of the Mediterranean.

The prey, whoever it was, had what they wanted—at least they thought they did—so what would they do next? That was what the brigadier knew, and that was what he was acting on.

He knew what they would do next.

A slow, cold, prickling dread came over me. I was telling

myself it could not be true, but the logic was relentless. And there was sweet FA I could do about it. I drained my glass and went inside. Powerlessness produces its own kind of panic. I felt sick, and my brain was racing, trying frantically to produce a course of action. Should I call Colonel Schwartz? Gordon? But I didn't know who I could trust.

I was about to reach for my phone when it rang. I grabbed it and saw a number I didn't recognize. Jane.

"Yeah?"

"There has been a weird development. I don't know what it means."

"Cavendish is flying to the Middle East."

"How the hell...?"

"Where to? How much do you know?"

"Syria. It's hard to know who to trust, Harry. I had someone tailing him. He is on his way to Syria as we speak. But he seems to be going incognito."

"Jane, can you get access to the president?"

"Christ, Harry!"

"Can you or not?"

"Yes, probably, with difficulty, but yes. I think so."

"Do it. Tell him everything, except the fact that the brigadier is alive. As far as you know, his body was identified. Then tell him what you told me. He'll probably work it out for himself, but if he doesn't, tell him this..."

I spelled it out for her. She was silent for a moment. Then she swore violently and hung up.

I called Colonel Gordon while I started to pack a rucksack. I was going to need his Grenadier.

# NINETEEN

THE STARS WERE ICE COLD, HIGH IN A TRANSLUCENT sky. We had crossed the southern end of the Golan Heights, fording the Ruqqad river and the following dirt tracks that wound through fertile farmland until we came suddenly to a series of harsh, steep hills that rose starkly on our right, to the north and east. Here Colonel Gordon stopped.

"From here on, you're on your own."

He opened the driver's door but stopped, staring at the black windshield.

"This is not a war, Mr. Bauer. This is *the* war. Evil has taken root in these lands. This is not a war for land or resources. This is the war for survival. This is good against evil. Do you understand that?"

After a while, I nodded. "Yeah, Colonel. I understand that."

"They don't understand what they are up against. They think it's business as usual. But it's not. This is different."

He swung down and walked back down the track toward the dark glint of the river. I climbed down too and went to the trunk. After a minute or so, I heard the quiet hum of a motor receding back toward Israel. I took out a set of magnetic Syrian plates, put them over the Israeli ones, and drove on along the track, making for the town of Ma'ariya. From there, it was a sixty mile drive through the night to Damascus.

Sixty miles from say, Oyster Bay to Southampton on Long Island is probably something you could do in an hour or less. But sixty miles from the fringes of the Golan Heights, through remote, winding dirt tracks among sprawling fields, followed by blacktop roads through cities on red alert against Israeli attacks on the one hand and jihadist attacks on the other, was going to take me from one a.m. until dawn, if I was lucky.

As it was, I arrived at Damascus International Airport at four a.m. The details the colonel had sent me said that Cavendish's private charter would land at eight-thirty in the morning, which gave me a little less than four hours to have some black coffee laced with whiskey, a cold hamburger in a bun, and three and a half hours' doze.

I awoke five minutes before my alarm went off. I had some more coffee and a stale bun, ran my fingers through my hair, and went in to use the men's lavatory. There I washed my face and combed my hair, and by the time I returned to the concourse, a uniformed driver was standing at arrivals with his hired muscle. That was what I expected, but I ignored them and went back out, making for the parking lot. Right outside the main entrance was their dark blue Audi with smoked windows. I paused to tie my bootlaces and slapped the tracking device into the rear wheel arch.

When I got back to the Grenadier, I moved the truck so I could pull out and follow them without making it too obvious.

At twenty past eight, a Gulfstream 700 came in to land and ten minutes later came to a halt outside the terminal.

Damascus Airport is basic, like most of Damascus. It has one terminal and looks like it was built in the early seventies. It took Cavendish and another guy in a suit just ten minutes more to get through with their driver and bodyguard. They climbed into the Audi and took off at speed, making the circle and moving straight onto the Damascus Airport Motorway. I followed, keeping my distance.

He drove fast, staying in the fast lane, through broad flatlands where sprawling farms slowly gave way to scattered, shabby suburbs. I was able to stay well back, following him on the screen. After less than ten minutes, we came to the big Jaraman interchange, surrounded by refugee camps that had become shantytowns populated by hungry, despairing victims of their own obsession with hatred and subjugation.

Here he made a big circle and came out headed west along Almotahalik Aljanobi. Two miles on, he came off the freeway and headed north along a broad, tree-lined avenue that had once been elegant and well maintained but was now shabby, dirty, and crumbling. A couple more turns through streets that spoke of despair and destitution and we were suddenly on a broad avenue that was just as filthy and unkempt as the rest of the city seemed to be, except that ahead of us, rising up gleaming white in the early sun like something out a movie by George Lucas was the stepped pyramid of the Four Seasons hotel.

The Audi pulled up at the main entrance, and I saw Cavendish and his pal exit the car and move toward the hotel before I turned right into Al Brazil and parked outside the Al Jalaa' Park. I called Jane on the last cell she'd used. She obviously hadn't thrown it away because she answered on the first ring.

"Yes?"

"You'd better book me into the Four Seasons in Damascus. Make it a suite. Cavendish just got dropped there from the airport."

"OK, give me ten minutes."

She hung up, and I took ten long minutes to pull out of the parking lot, cruise up the hotel entrance park, and walk up to the big glass doors. The doorman made a face like it was a pity I was there. I might prefer somewhere else.

"Have you a reservation, sir? I'm afraid we are all full."

I gave him twenty bucks and said, "Yeah, I have a reservation. I just got mugged, and I am not happy. Get valet parking to take care of my car, will you."

At the reception desk, a pretty girl with a scarf over her head smiled at me like I must be lost.

"I have a reservation. Harry Bauer. A suite. I just got mugged, so I am going to need a bottle of Bushmills, a pot of coffee, and a shower. And have a valet bring up what luggage I've got left from my car." I gave her the registration. "By the way, can you tell me if my friend Charles Cavendish has arrived? We arranged to meet here today."

She smiled, reassured that I was the kind of person they wanted at the Four Seasons.

"Yes, sir. He has just checked in to the presidential suite. Would you like me to call him for you?"

"No, no, I need a drink and a shower. Then I'll call him."

I went up and had a long shower. The valet brought my leather bag, and I changed into a fresh pair of Wranglers and a clean shirt. As I drank my coffee, I called down to have them bring up my car. I had a background anxiety that they might leave in a different vehicle.

It was a guy on reception. He smiled at me as I approached. I gave him my registration number and asked for the keys. As he handed them over, I asked him, "Has Mr. Cavendish come down yet?" I grinned. "I'm hoping to get to the restaurant before him."

"No, Mr. Cavendish is still in his suite."

I went out, got my car, and parked beside the gardens next door with my side mirror focused on the hotel entrance and the screen switched on, showing no activity with the Audi. I looked at my watch. It was just after eleven a.m. By eleven-thirty I was telling myself it could be a long wait, when the light on the screen started winking and a few moments later, the dark Audi came out of the underground parking lot and stopped at the front entrance. A couple of minutes after that, Cavendish and his pal trotted out and got in the back of the car. It pulled away, accelerated, and drove past me, headed west. I pulled out and went after them, keeping my distance.

At the Umayyad Square, which is actually a large circle with seven roads radiating from a central fountain, they took the fifth exit onto Fayez Mansour, a three-mile, tree-lined avenue which took us to Highway 1. They joined the highway, and I lagged behind, letting them pull well ahead. It wasn't hard; they were going fast, and the road was straight and almost empty.

After a couple of miles or so, we started a steady climb up into the Anti-Lebanon Mountains. The terrain was dry, arid, and rocky. It wasn't hard to imagine it as the home of an angry, vengeful god. I would be glad to get back to the fertile, generous greens of New York and New England.

If I ever did.

We climbed for about seven miles, moving steadily north and a little west through apocalyptic landscapes of red and gray and small villages baked in the sun in the fragile shade of small, withered trees.

Then, quite suddenly, we arrived at As'Saboura. The small village was on the right. On the left was the sprawling, luxurious suburb of Yafour, where it seemed every house was a palace and every building that was not a palatial home was a luxurious restaurant, bar, or café. It made you wonder where the waiters, servants, and cleaners lived, until you realized they lived on the other side of Highway 1, in As'Saboura.

The Audi slowed, came off the highway, and looped under it to enter the sprawl of super-luxury villas half-hidden among an abundance of trees, flowering bushes, and palms. I followed, allowing the distance between us to expand so I was not visible in their rearview mirror.

They wound their way among streets laid out on a grid system until, at the far northern extreme of the town, they came to a massive, sprawling piece of real estate that took up an entire block. At a guess, looking at it on my screen, I figured it must be eight or nine acres.

I pulled over half a mile from where the Audi had gone in, in the shade of some tall cypress trees, and found some satellite imagery of the area. It wasn't real clear, but it was clear enough, and it was no exaggeration to describe the place as a palace. The house itself, with patios, gardens, pools, fountains, and mother-in-law wings, covered an area of two and a half acres, the size of a small farm. That was just the house. It stood at the far eastern end of the property. From there to the road, there stretched another five acres of gardens and orchards, bisected by a tree-lined drive. To get onto that drive, you had to go through an iron gate supported by two huge towers surmounted by battlements.

Common sense dictated that a house like that had tight—and lethal—security. There would be armed men, dogs, cameras, sensors, and anything else they could dream up, like heat-detecting lasers and a remote-controlled bridge over piranha-infested waters. And a guy that said things like, "Ve do not tolerate failure, Mr. Bont!"

I reflected for a moment on the irony of the situation. I was here to save and protect the brigadier, largely because he had guided me and taught me so much. And among the main things he had taught was never undertake a job without a good plan based on sufficient, reliable intelligence.

Looked like this was going to be the job that proved he was right.

I figured I had to allow myself one drive-by. That was as much reconnaissance as I could do. After that I had to act.

Ignoring the question, "Act how, Harry?" that was knocking on the inside of my skull, I drove slowly to the end of the road. The two towers and the huge, iron gate were fronted by a paved parking lot with room for ten or twelve cars. At each tower, there was a guy in uniform with an assault rifle.

I scouted around the area for a while, counting the number of security cameras attached to walls, gates, and posts. There were a lot. I noticed they were all on private property. There were none on street lamps or utility poles. There were none on public buildings because there didn't appear to be any public buildings. An idea began to germinate in my brain, and when I saw the cell phone tower on a hill behind what seemed to be a small cop shop, it began to take definite shape. It would be suicide, but I had already resigned myself to that. This might just work.

I pulled in to the small police station, killed the engine, and climbed out. I noted there was one small Honda 4X4. I stepped in through the door like I had serious business there and saw two guys sitting at desks behind a counter. They both scowled at me. A third guy sat behind the counter manning a computer. He scowled at me too. A fourth was leaning against the wall reading a magazine. He was the one who spoke, shouting, letting off a stream of ugly noises at me that sounded like "*Inta min? Shu biddack? Ma fiik tfuut la hoon!*"

I frowned at him and said, "Osama bin Laden?"

That stopped them all dead in their mental tracks and gave me enough time to pull the BULL SAS from under my arm and plug the guy who was standing between the eyes. That took about half a second. The guy sitting behind the counter went down in the other half of that second, with a slug through his right eye. The two at the back off the office took a little longer because they had started to move. In four seconds it was all over.

The guy who'd been standing was roughly my size. I took his shirt and his pants and put them on. I scrounged around and found the keys to the 4X4 and went out to transfer my rucksack from the Grenadier to the Honda, climbed behind the wheel, and made my way unchallenged to the cell tower, about half a mile away. I stopped in back of the building, where I was less visible, and opened up the rucksack Colonel Gordon had arranged for me. The man was like Santa Claus after binge-watching Arnold Schwarzenegger movies.

I took out four cakes of C4 of the ten he'd packed and a couple of detonators. I packed two of them around the base of the antenna itself and plugged in the detonator. Then I walked around to the door of the cabin, blew out the lock, and packed another two cakes against the telecom equipment inside.

After that, I drove back down the hill toward Yafour and the palatial house where Cavendish was being entertained. As I pulled into the parking lot, I dialed eight and nine on my cell, and there was a loud though distant bang and a smack in the air. The two guards who had been looking at me and the police

4X4 now looked up and around, searching for the source of the bang.

I climbed out and walked toward them, carrying the rucksack. The nearest one started jerking his chin at me and barking in Ugly, like he was clearing his throat. I kept walking toward his pal and gestured to him to follow. My expression said he was in trouble. He was. When I had them a couple of feet away, I said, "Do you know who I am?"

Clearly a Syrian cop in a Syrian police vehicle speaking to them in English was something that required several seconds to process. Those were the seconds I used to drive the Fairbairn and Sykes through both their throats. It was messy, but it stopped them shouting or raising the alert. As they lay dying by the gate, I told them, "Apparently, I am the Reaper of Zion."

# TWENTY

I MOVED QUICKLY ALONG THE DRIVE, PAST THE orchards and the gardens, and broke into a jog as I approached the sprawling, marble edifice, festooned with arches and domes, like something out of a thousand and one nights. Ahead of me, at the top of a sweep of semi-circular steps fashioned into the shape of mollusks, there was a huge arch with two massive wooden doors held up by passive hinges and encrusted with bronze studs. Within those double doors was another set of more prosaic double doors made of wood at the bottom and glass panels at the top.

I rapped on that with my knuckles, and after a moment, I saw a guy in an expensive suit with a collarless shirt approaching. He was frowning at his cell as he walked. When he glanced up, I showed him my phone and pointed at it. So now it made some kind of sense to him that a cop had been allowed to get as far as the front door because there was some problem with the phones.

He opened the door with an ugly expression on his face, jerked his chin at me, and said, "*Shu biddak?*"

I still had the cell held up in my right hand. I said, "My shoe is fine," and slammed the edge of the phone into the bridge of his nose. I didn't want him shouting, so as he bent forward gripping his nose, I let the Fairbairn and Sykes slip from my sleeve into my hand and rammed it into the side of his neck. I let him die and lowered him to the floor before I removed the blade.

I wiped the blade on his Armani jacket, slipped it into my boot, and extracted the X-95 from the rucksack along with the grenade launcher. I paused and listened but heard nothing but distant voices echoing on marble. They had that scandalized tone people get when they are deprived of the Internet or their cell phone.

I took the suppressor from my rucksack and screwed it onto the BUL, then started moving forward with the semi automatic held out in front of me and the assault rifle hanging from my shoulder.

I was in an ample, domed hall with a blue marble floor and turquoise marble walls. There were lots of potted palms and ferns and a fountain playing in the center. Four corridors branched off, two on the right and two on the left. In the center, a broad marble staircase rose and split into ram's horns curling away into a gallery above.

I made for the second corridor on my left based on the unsupported intuitive belief that it led to the back of the house, and that was where I would find the most useful people. As it turned out, I wasn't wrong. I quickly came to an office on my right. There were four men in it, and they all had their cells out and were gesticulating. One was sitting behind a desk. A guy in uniform was standing. The other two were in expensive suits and had that military look you never really lose. They looked startled when I appeared in the doorway. I put my finger to my lips, stepped in, and kicked the door closed with my heel. I wracked my memory and came up with, "*Hal bithki ingleezi?*" which as far as I could remember meant *Do you speak English?* in Arabic.

I had seconds, if that. None of them answered. They just stared with astonished faces. In half a second I decided the guy in uniform was the least likely, and the two ex militaries came a close second. I shot the three of them at point blank range in a second and a half, making a mess of the walls. Into the fourth second I had the BUL trained on the guy behind the desk. He'd gone pasty and had his hands up. He looked upper middle class and educated. If any one of them spoke English, it was going to be him. I smiled.

"There is a right answer and there is a wrong answer. Get it wrong and you die. Get it right and you live. Do you speak English?"

He swallowed hard. "Yes, a little."

"Right answer. Now what is your name?"

"Ali."

"OK, Ali, we are making progress. Now I guess you are an administrator, and you don't go around killing people, raping women, or inciting war. Am I right?"

"Yes, you are right. I am just administrator, manager, I don't—"

"That's fine, Ali. You see, I am basically a nice guy. I don't like killing people unless they really deserve it. You're probably a nice guy, wife and kids, you don't want to hurt anyone, right?"

"Yes, please."

"So I'll tell you what I am going to do. You tell me where the American, Mr. Cavendish, is. I let you go home, and I tell the CIA and the Mossad how helpful you were and not to come after you."

His pupils had become pinpricks, and he seemed to have become paralyzed. He was in a double bind, and his brain had shut down. I clicked my fingers.

"Ali, you need to react, pal." He had a glass of water on his desk. I picked it up and splashed it in his face. He gasped, startled. "We have an Israeli invasion of Damascus starting in two hours. You don't want to be caught in this palace, friend. You need to go home and take your family out of the city. I am going to inform my superiors you collaborated. Understand? The alternative is I shoot you. I don't want to do that. Are you understanding this, Ali?"

He was nodding now, trying to control his growing panic. Yes, yes. I collaborate!"

"Where is Cavendish?"

He pointed. "Last door on the left. Big dining room."

"How many people?"

He seemed to panic for a moment, then closed his eyes and focused. "Murhaf Abu Qasra, Minister of Defense, Anas Khattab, Minister of Interior, Farhad Ahmadi, representative from Iran, and Iran Minister of Foreign Affairs, Hossein Amir Abdollahian. Also American President Cavendish and personal secretary La Valle."

It was true I didn't want to kill him, but neither could I let him go. So I smacked him on the jaw and told him to be grateful. It could have been a lot worse.

I opened the door and went to step out. I saw, twenty feet away, ten guys down on one knee with rifles at their shoulders. I ducked back as a hundred and fifty rounds tore into the door and the wall at he the back of the office, showering plaster and wood splinters among spitting, ricocheting lead.

I heard a shout and tramping boots as they closed in. I didn't wait. I slipped an RPG in the launcher, hunkered down, and fired the grenade into their midst just fifteen feet away. I heard that horrible, flat smack of the report and scrambled out and down the corridor toward where Ali had told me the meeting was taking place. Behind me I could hear pitiful screams and weeping. There were other sounds, shouts of anger and orders to come after me.

Ahead of me a tall, walnut door opened, and four guys in uniform burst out with their weapons at their shoulders. I had already slipped in a second grenade, and now I fired before they could take up positions. I fell to the ground, waiting for the explosion. I let off two controlled bursts at those chasing me, another two at anyone who might be left standing ahead of me, scrabbled to my feet, and hurtled the remaining fifteen feet toward the big walnut door that still stood open. There was a rattle behind me, and rounds hit the walls and the door as I ducked in.

There were the six men he said would be there, but there were six armed guards too.

I slammed the door behind me and bellowed at the people gathered inside, pointing the X-95 at them, "*Up against the far wall! Now! Now!*"

I rammed a detonator into a cake of C4, dropped it at the base of the door, and bellowed at the company again, "*Back! Back! Back!*" as I advanced on them. They knew what was coming and scrambled over each other to get as far from the door as they could. Some crawled under the table, some hid behind chairs. I could see Cavendish, staring at me like I was crazy and hiding behind his personal secretary.

The doors burst open, and I pressed 9 on my cell. It was grotesque. Fifteen men were vaporized into pink mist among which bits of limbs spun and jumped in ways that seemed deeply and disturbingly wrong. The doors were ripped from their hinges and smashed against the walls.

Then there was a ringing, sickening silence.

I got to my feet and stared at Cavendish. He was trembling, sitting on the floor behind his secretary. I was about to speak but heard a horrible screeching howl of rage from behind me. My rucksack was dragged from my shoulder, taking the X-95 with it. I turned and had the strange sensation of things happening in slow motion. I could see a man in traditional Arabic dress, his robes flowing softly as he swung a gleaming scimitar in both hands. Behind him, bizarrely, I registered the spot on the wall from which he had snatched it. The razor sharp blade was maybe a quarter of a second from my throat. If he had gone for my belly, he would have killed me, but I leaned back, and the point skimmed my shirt, tearing it.

As he came for the return backhander, I sprang forward, pinning his right arm against his body with my left hand, and rammed my right index finger into his right eye. His scream turned to one of pain and terror. I took the sword from his hand, swung it in both hands, and took off his head.

Then it was havoc and mayhem. Eleven men all storming but not sure if they were storming me or the door to get out. There were the armed guards waving their guns but reluctant to shoot in case they killed a minister or a foreign dignitary. And then there was me, possessed by a sudden, insane rage, piling into them as they surged forward.

A guard came at me with his semi-automatic, his face twisted with excitement because he had a clear shot. I came down and across and took off his arm. He went down spraying blood, his heart pumping overtime. I took a step to my right and decapitated the Minister of Defense. As his head spun in the air, I brought the blade down vertically through the Minister of the Interior's skull and split his head down to his collar bone. I felt arms encircle my waist. Others went around my neck. They were pulling at me, but the rage was uncontrollable.

I flipped the sword so the blade was facing down and stabbed savagely behind me. I felt warm blood gush over my leg. A fist struck my face, and I brought the blade arcing up. The blade bit into a guard's groin, splitting his hip and his tendons, and he want down. I could still feel the arms around my waist. Ahead, five men were backing away from me, but the weight of a man was pulling me back. I gripped the arm with my left hand and rammed the blade, point first into his armpit, heard him gasp, and felt him fall away.

Then I surged forward. There were two guards, an Iranian, Cavendish, and his man. The guards now had a clear shot, but I was moving too fast. I swung to the left, and a hand clutching a sidearm spun in the air, trailing a spray of blood. I swung to the right. The pistol exploded. My arm burned, but I didn't notice. The blade bit into his belly, and he fell, disemboweled, to the blue, marble floor in a spreading pool of crimson blood.

The Iranian was running, but he never stood a chance. I caught him in two strides and took off his head in one single sweep. Then I turned and strode toward Cavendish. The terror in his face showed that he could read what was in mine. La Valle came toward me with his hands clenched like he was praying. He said something about being American. I didn't listen. I took off his head too, and stood over Cavendish.

"Why the hit on the brigadier?"

His face creased, and he started to weep. "What?"

"Why did you abduct the brigadier and order the hit on him?" All he could do was look around him at the carnage. I said, "He had information about your frauds and the people you'd had killed because they were a threat."

His voice was barely a whisper. "Yes..."

"And you thought by framing the abduction as an Israeli operation, you could further turn public and political opinion against Israel and allow Iran to recover its nuclear program, in which you and your foundation are heavily invested. Is that correct?"

He was frowning at me like I was insane, like I didn't make sense. He said, "Yes... Who *are* you? What have you done?"

"*Yes or no?*"

"Yes!"

"You tried to secure your own credentials with Cobra by asking for a hit on the ayatollah. A hit you knew would never be carried out because you had arranged to have the brigadier eliminated. And you figured by making him a victim of Israel, any material that was revealed about you as a result of the brigadier's insurance you could discredit as an Israeli fraud, probably by the Mossad. It was you and your contacts in Hamas who gave Colonel Gordon the intelligence to allow the rescue of the hostages so that he would turn a blind eye to your abduction of the brigadier. But you never intended the rescue operation to be successful. It was supposed to be a failure so Israel could be accused of incompetently breaching the ceasefire."

He had started weeping. "How do you know all this? What the hell happens to me now? Who the hell *are* you?"

"Who am I? They tell me I'm the Reaper of Zion. What happens to you now? Pal, you get reaped!"

I took off his head with a single sweep. Then I crossed the blood-drenched dining room toward the corridor. I knew there was no way I was going to make it out of Syria. But I didn't care. I had done what I came to do. Now they could take me and shoot me. I was done. My only regret, and I smiled with some irony as I thought of the cell tower, was that I would never know what had become of the brigadier.

He was smart and resourceful, among the best of the best. He'd make it somehow. I had secured a promise from Colonel Gordon that they would look out for him and make sure he was safe.

I crossed the massive entrance hall. Behind me, I could hear stampeding feet and shouting voices. I ignored them, dropped the rucksack and the weapons as I walked, and climbed into the large fountain, where I submerged myself and washed away all the blood. As the water turned red, I emerged and splashed water over my face.

The sudden scream of jets made me look up. Two Israeli F-35s thundered overhead, and in the distance I heard explosions, but they were drowned out by the thudding of helicopter rotors. Two UH-60 Blackhawks were closing in. One opened up on the palace door, while a guy leaned out of the other and beckoned me toward the orchards. I ran.

Thirty seconds later, soaking wet, I was being hoisted up into the chopper, we were banking and, accompanied by the second helicopter, close behind, we hurtled south and west, toward the Golan Heights and Israel.

Two guys helped me to a seat and strapped me in as I wiped water from my eyes and my hair. "I was never so glad to see anyone in..."

I trailed off. Sitting opposite me was the brigadier, smiling. He reached into his pocket and pulled out a hipflask and handed it over to me.

"You're bleeding from your arm and from your belly," he said. "And I should have thought you would know by now that every effective operation must have a good extraction plan. Thank heavens I happened to show up to get you out of trouble."

I started to say, "Where...?" but decided to take a long pull on the whiskey instead. When I was done, he said, "Where was I? I have numerous friends in Tel Aviv. I called one and had him come and pick me up. I didn't want to broadcast that I was alive and well, but I had put two and two together that Cavendish was arranging something with Syria and Iran. I made contact with the Mossad, arranged a meeting, and they told me you were well ahead of me, but you hadn't arranged extraction."

I nodded for a while, watching the dry, burned sand slide past below.

"Did you call Jane? She was..." I kept staring at the dry, dry desert below. "She was hit real hard. Does she know you're OK?"

He nodded but didn't say anything. I shrugged and attempted a smile. "Thanks for coming to get me."

"I was going to say the same thing."

And we flew on in silence.

# EPILOGUE

I HAD GONE TO SEE MIRIAM TO SAY GOODBYE. Colonel Benjamin Gordon was there. The visit had lasted just five minutes. Miriam had been very quiet. The colonel and I had done most of the talking, and he had embraced me when I left and told me I would always have a home in Israel.

It was a long flight back. I hadn't stopped in New York or DC. I hadn't gone to see Jane, the colonel. Something told me she and the brigadier had a lot to talk about. Instead I had flown to Jackson Hole. I had collected my Grand Cherokee from the long-term parking and had driven through the early morning down to Pinedale.

As I had turned into Pole Creek Road and crested the hill, the mighty Wind River Mountains had risen up, tall and misty, powerful and peaceful and timeless. I smiled as I cruised along toward my mountain home in Wyoming, the last sane place on Earth, and thought of that other Miriam, whose free soul and spirit now lived among the pines and the rocks and the cascading creeks.

I pulled in to my long drive, left the truck out front,

poured myself a generous Bushmills, though the sun was not yet over the yardarm, and sat myself on my rocking chair on the deck to look across the great valley to Half Moon Mountain and the great snowy peaks of the Winds.

"Here's to you," I said, "Miriam."

**Don't miss JUSTICE WITHOUT MERCY. The riveting sequel in the Harry Bauer Thriller series.**

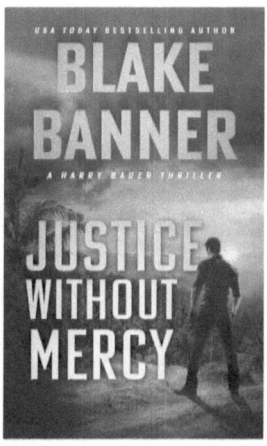

Scan the QR code below to purchase
JUSTICE WITHOUT MERCY.

Or go to: righthouse.com/justice-without-mercy

# DON'T MISS ANYTHING!

If you want to stay up to date on all new releases in this series, with this author, or with any of our new deals, you can do so by joining our newsletters below.

In addition, you will immediately gain access to our entire *Right House VIP Library,* which includes many riveting Mystery and Thriller novels for your enjoyment!

righthouse.com/email

*(Easy to unsubscribe. No spam. Ever.)*

# ALSO BY BLAKE BANNER

Up to date books can be found at:
www.righthouse.com/blake-banner

## ROGUE THRILLERS
Gates of Hell (Book 1)
Hell's Fury (Book 2)
Ice Burn (Book 3)
Judgement by Fire (Book 4)

## ALEX MASON THRILLERS
Odin (Book 1)
Ice Cold Spy (Book 2)
Mason's Law (Book 3)
Assets and Liabilities (Book 4)
Russian Roulette (Book 5)
Executive Order (Book 6)
Dead Man Talking (Book 7)
All The King's Men (Book 8)
Flashpoint (Book 9)
Brotherhood of the Goat (Book 10)
Dead Hot (Book 11)
Blood on Megiddo (Book 12)
Son of Hell (Book 13)
Merchant of Death (Book 14)
Extinction C-14 (Book 15)
A Vengeful God (Book 16)

## HARRY BAUER THRILLER SERIES
Dead of Night (Book 1)

Dying Breath (Book 2)

The Einstaat Brief (Book 3)

Quantum Kill (Book 4)

Immortal Hate (Book 5)

The Silent Blade (Book 6)

LA: Wild Justice (Book 7)

Breath of Hell (Book 8)

Invisible Evil (Book 9)

The Shadow of Ukupacha (Book 10)

Sweet Razor Cut (Book 11)

Blood of the Innocent (Book 12)

Blood on Balthazar (Book 13)

Simple Kill (Book 14)

Riding The Devil (Book 15)

The Unavenged (Book 16)

The Devil's Vengeance (Book 17)

Bloody Retribution (Book 18)

Rogue Kill (Book 19)

Blood for Blood (Book 20)

The Cell (Book 21)

Time to Die (Book 22)

The Reaper of Zion (Book 23)

Justice Without Mercy (Book 24)

## DEAD COLD MYSTERY SERIES
An Ace and a Pair (Book 1)

Two Bare Arms (Book 2)

Garden of the Damned (Book 3)

Let Us Prey (Book 4)

The Sins of the Father (Book 5)

## THE OMEGA SERIES

# ABOUT US

Right House is an independent publisher created by authors for readers. We specialize in Action, Thriller, Mystery, and Crime novels.

If you enjoyed this novel, then there is a good chance you will like what else we have to offer! Please stay up to date by using any of the links below.

Join our mailing lists to stay up to date -->
righthouse.com/email
Visit our website --> righthouse.com
Contact us --> contact@righthouse.com

facebook.com/righthousebooks
x.com/righthousebooks
instagram.com/righthousebooks

# EXCLUSIVE SNEAK PEEK OF...

**JUSTICE WITHOUT MERCY**

# CHAPTER 1

CAN VENGEANCE BE ANY PART OF JUSTICE? THERE are plenty of people in this broken world who will tell you that if a guy breaks into your house and rapes, mutilates, and murders your daughter or your wife, you should engage in a meaningful dialogue with him, to discover what deep pain or sense of dispossession led him to do it—like his motivation makes what he did somehow OK.

And maybe you should even consider that what he did is actually your fault. For existing in the first place.

I am not a philosopher or a lawyer, but I know that justice is about balance, and so is vengeance. This a cruel world where in order simply to survive, we have to eat each other. Literally, not figuratively. In that kind of world, when your daughter or your wife has been raped, mutilated, and murdered, meaningful dialogue will not bring them back. But it will allow the bastard who killed them to believe he can do it again and do what the hell he likes and get away with it. Blowing his brains out will not bring them back either, but it will stop him doing it to anybody else, and it will let his pals know that hurting innocent people has consequences.

That is about the extent of my philosophy.

I had been thinking about that kind of stuff for a couple of months at my log cabin in Pinedale, Wyoming. I'd been sitting on my deck, taking a rest, looking at the Wind River Mountains across the plain, watching the mustang running half-wild in the fields below my house on the hill. Earlier, I'd been chopping wood for the long winter ahead, and while I did all those things, I had been telling myself it was time to accept the fact that little Miriam had gone from this world[1]. She had found her peace and was no longer a ghost who haunted me and drove me to revenge; and Dr. Claire Erickson was no longer the woman who was going to rescue me from my darkness[2].

I was a killer. Colonel Gordon of the IDF had called me *Mal'akh ha-Neqamah*, the angel of vengeance. And if I never killed another man again in what was left of my life, I would still always be nothing but a killer. It's what I am: an angel of death.

It was into this private, hermetic world that Brigadier Alexander 'Buddy' Byrd drove on the early afternoon of Monday, September 15th. I was sitting on the fence, watching the mustang and wondering which one I was going to take for my own, when I saw a silver Cherokee pull into the drive a quarter of a mile down the hill. It took its time grinding its way up the track and ground to a halt as I swung down from the fence. The driver's window was open, and as I approached, I saw it was the brigadier. He smiled.

"Got a drink for a weary traveler?"

---

1. See *Reaper of Zion*
2. See *The Devil's Revenge* and *Time to Die*

"No, but I have got a couple of drinks and a bison steak, if you're man enough."

He laughed, and I followed him up the drive and across the small wooden bridge over the creek in front of my house. There I climbed onto the deck that runs around my house and made for the fridge, while he parked his truck out back by the kitchen door. That was where I met him with a cold bottle of beer.

"Very welcome," he said and drained half of it on the doorstep. He dumped a leather Gladstone bag by the stairs and wiped his mouth on his sleeve. "You're pretty remote up here. Got somewhere I can crash for the night?"

I smiled. "Sure, you can sleep in the stable with the horses, as long as you don't snore. They're light sleepers." I moved over to the fridge and pulled out a couple of steaks. "I've got four bedrooms up those stairs. Mine's the one with a P226 hanging from the bedpost. Take your pick of the other three."

He drained the last of his beer, muttered something about being better off with the horses, and carried his bag upstairs.

Twenty minutes later, we were seated at the big hunk of polished redwood that served me as a table, and the brigadier paused in his eating to lean back and glance at me while he put his napkin to his mouth.

"Harry, we have a delicate matter to discuss."

"The colonel says I blew up too many things, and now you want me to take early retirement.[3]"

He chuckled. "Even Jane is coming to understand that you only blow things up when you absolutely have to. Which, I confess, seems to be most of the time. No, I don't want you to take early retirement. Neither does she, for that matter. Quite

---

3. See, e.g. *Immortal Hate* and *The Silent Blade*

the contrary, but I do want you to go a little beyond the usual Cobra brief."

I nodded down at the bison sirloin on my plate. "So is this a Cobra brief? Or is it a private enterprise?"

He sighed and examined his glass of Muga, like the answer to my question was in there somewhere.

"A bit of both. Let us say it starts as a private enterprise, and depending on the intelligence you gather, it might become a Cobra brief."

"OK."

"We have received reports which we need to confirm." He paused and gave what he'd just said some thought. "Who is we?" he said. "The answer to that is confidential, so let's say I. I want you to take not early retirement but a holiday. If on that holiday you can confirm that the reports we have are accurate, then the Cobra brief will become active."

"What are those reports?"

He nodded, like he agreed with the question. "You know that lithium is rare and extremely expensive."

I echoed his nod. "Sure."

"There are few places on Earth where it can be found, and its value to..." He paused and arched an eyebrow at me. "Its value to defense contractors is incalculable. The American war machine is the deadliest, most powerful machine this planet has seen in fifteen thousand years. But take away its electronic capabilities, and the entire military industrial *intelligence* complex of the Western world becomes very vulnerable indeed."

"So we are talking about mining."

He nodded rather ponderously. "Partly. We are talking about an *alleged* mining operation on a small island nobody has ever heard of."

I frowned. "OK, where is that?"

"St. Homer." He glanced at me. "That's with an H, like the Greek poet. The origin of the name may have been a joke originally because the native inhabitants back in the sixteenth century were the I-Takka tribe who spoke a dialect of Lokono. They called the island I-Takka, which in their dialect might mean stone or, as it is spelt, it could mean 'I go.' Nobody is left who speaks that dialect, so we shall never know. However, Itaca in Spanish, pronounced as in Greek ee-taca, refers to Ithaca, Odysseus' homeland. So St. Homer with an H might have been an erudite joke. Or it might refer to the seventh century bishop, St. Audomar, who was also known as St. Omer..."

He trailed off, having apparently lost his thread. I said, "We shall never know."

"Quite. We shall never know. However, the island, which is just seven miles long and three across at its widest point, lies some seventy miles off the Atlantic coast of South America, precisely between Guyana and Surinam. Both countries lay claim to it, but neither has been willing to make any kind of military move to take possession of it, lest it be perceived as provocative. The claims went to arbitration back in the late '70s. They were overseen by the United States, but that process seemed to stagnate round about the time Mr. Stanley Whittingham's work on the lithium battery got seriously underway at Exxon. Nobody since then has seemed terribly keen to kick-start it again, either."

"Is that odd?"

"Maybe. There are inhabitants on the island. There is a city hall, apparently, but it is pretty basic. There is no formal census of the population, as you'd imagine, but estimates put it at about two thousand people, probably more. They are a mix of Portuguese, Spanish, French, native Indians, and descendants of African slaves. As far as we can tell, there are three towns, one of which is a functioning port, Puerto Ste. Maria. There is a town hall—what you would call City Hall—in Es Arenal, the capital of the island. Nobody pays income tax, or any kind of tax for that matter, so there is a question mark over how the town hall is funded."

"What about law enforcement?"

"Apparently there is a sheriff, but one has to ask, if there are no taxes, who pays him and his deputies? Who pays for the office and the gas in their trucks?"

He took a deep breath. "And the key issue here is that there *might* be a mine somewhere on the island, producing lithium for interests within—"

"The military industrial intelligence complex. And that mine is paying for the administration of City Hall and, most important, law enforcement. I.e., they own the island and the people on it."

"Precisely."

I ate for a moment in silence, then asked, "Why is that a problem? Why might it concern Cobra? Even if we disapprove of some of their methods"—I gave a small shrug—"or even their existence, we are a part of the military industrial intelligence complex. We need them, and they need us."

"That's true, in the abstract. But all too often, that complex ends up perpetrating everything we exist to fight against."

"Crimes against humanity."

"There are pieces"—he shook his head, searching for accurate words—"elements such as minerals, chips, processors—thousands of different parts—that go into American and NATO armaments and defense technologies that were mined or made by abused and exploited people. It is an industry that by its very nature *must be* amoral. So it is very difficult to decide where to draw the line. What abuses and exploitations you are going to..." He paused and took a deep breath. He didn't like the words available to him. "I'm not going to say turn a blind eye to. We don't. We can't. We know what is happening in those mines and factories, but the price of taking action is too high. It would damage our defense industry and make us too vulnerable."

I nodded that I understood. "The extremes are clear. You can't execute a man for shouting at an employee or paying him a poor wage. You can't not execute a man who enslaves, rapes, tortures, and murders children, but as you narrow the gap, where do you draw the line? Where does it become unacceptable?"

"Precisely. What we do is accept and tolerate because our position as the most powerful military in the world necessarily depends on that industry."

He sipped his wine, and as he set down his glass, he produced a rueful smile.

"It's a funny thing, though. Even if it is hard sometimes to know what we will tolerate. When it comes down to it, we know exactly what we *won't* tolerate. Those things you listed: child slavery—any kind of slavery but especially child slavery— is intolerable. Rape and sexual abuse, torture and murder, are beyond what we can tolerate if we are to remain human. And *if* what we have been told is accurate, all of these things are going on at the mine."

He wiped his mouth with his napkin and dropped it on the table.

"I say that," he went on, "but we don't even know for sure that there is a mine."

"Satellite imagery?"

"There is something there, but exactly what it is is unclear. It seems there is some kind of electromagnetic field interfering with the satellite images."

I leaned back in my chair and crossed my arms. "But there must be bills of lading, contracts of sale, shipping documents, some kind of electronic or paper trail that indicates tons of lithium are being purchased—"

"That is very logical, and of course it's the first thing we looked at, but for a start, we are dealing with very obstructive, secretive defense contractors. These are departments and organizations that tell Congress to go to hell. In the second place, in many cases, this lithium winds up in places like Cabinda Itumbe or Mozambique, in Africa, or Malaysia and Singapore in Asia, or Buru, in Indonesia. In remote, deeply corrupt places like that, its origin becomes impossible to trace; and in the third place, as I mentioned earlier, I-Takka's jurisdiction is not so much not clear as non-existent. There is no legislature and therefore, technically, no law. And nobody is in a hurry to bring either into existence. So the laws governing shipping from the Port of Santa Maria are equally nonexistent. What leaves the Port of Santa Maria in those container ships is sometimes ambiguous to the point of absurdity. I have seen entries like 'mineral cargo' 'raw goods,' and even 'various.' So paper trails and electronic trails lead invariably down blind allies."

"So you need boots and eyes on the ground. What exactly do you want me to do?"

"As you can imagine, assuming there is any truth in the allegations, if Central Intelligence investigates, they will return having found no evidence at all because they serve the military industrial intelligence complex completely. They were virtually created by the same act of Congress.

"However, Cobra can't commission intelligence gathering.

That is well beyond its remit. So what I am asking you to do is totally unofficial. All I ask is that you go on holiday."

"They have infrastructure for that? Hotels, beach resorts...?"

"Oh, yes. They have hotels, bars, restaurants. It's not a place that is frequented much, so it's pretty basic, but if it turns out to be a false lead, you can at least have an enjoyable holiday on Cobra. We owe you a good rest."

"OK, I'll be happy to do that."

"I have a map of the island, documents, cash, all that stuff. But essentially you'll find the island has three large hills covered in dense pine forests on the far western extreme. As you head east and south toward Puerto Santa Maria, the island flattens out, and there are areas of gorse, moss, and bare rocks that form rocky cliffs jutting into the ocean. The center of the island, however, is made up of dense, fertile pine forest which thins out toward the east into what I can only describe as rolling downs. Beyond them is another area of hard, rocky cliffs that juts out into the sea with a lighthouse at the end. The intelligence we have indicates that this is the area where the mine is, on the North Faro Road."

"Hotels, car rentals..."

"All that information is in the file which I'll give you when you make the coffee and break out some of your excellent Irish single malt. I would like you to study it and decide how you want to approach it. After all, you are just going on holiday. You have nothing to hide, no hidden agenda..." He spread his hands.

I nodded. "Sure. Let's do it. I'll make the coffee."

# CHAPTER 2

We landed at Cheddi Jagan International Airport at nine a.m. local time. It was small enough to still be human. You could walk across the tarmac to the terminal building and deal with customs and passport control right there in the main hall, in full view of the plate glass windows and the country outside, without going through a single tunnel.

A guy from the British embassy with floppy, sandy hair was there. He shook hands warmly with a firm grip like he was really pleased to meet me.

"Mr. Bauer, I'm Andy, good to meet you, welcome to Guyana. We have a car outside..." He guided me toward the exit. "I'd offer you a lift to the port, but Buddy asked us to keep a low profile. However, we *do* have a few goodies for you in the boot. That's the trunk to you. Going to I-Takka, I understand. We've been keeping an eye on the place for a while."

"Have you got anyone over there?"

"Sadly, no. Our administration is in the hands of morons at the moment, I'm afraid. They think the way to make Britain great again is to cut all investment that brings a benefit or a yield and invest only in the black hole of social benefits for unqualified immigrants."

I laughed. "Hey, don't hold back on my account. Say what you really mean."

"Quite." He chuckled. "You know, make England—as opposed to Britain—great again, as an acronym, becomes MEGA. I think that's rather good, don't you? Here we are..."

I smiled as he opened the trunk of an old Bentley. "That's pretty good," I said. "It might even happen one day, when you stop hating yourselves."

He pulled out a Gladstone bag and set it at my feet.

"Quite. Mr. Bauer. I don't know what you're going to find on I-Takka. I *should* know, because it probably affects the balance of power on this planet, but our politicians are far too busy trying to get reelected and pursuing their own, sad little share of power instead of protecting our sacred Western values. Spain faced the same problem in 1936, and that resulted in a civil war that was the first ripple of the most devastating global war the world had ever seen." He smiled. "I am an historian, Mr. Bauer. History, like garlic, repeats itself. I hope I am wrong, but I fear we are about to see a very nasty belch, with the UK in the role of Spain."

By the time he'd finished, I was frowning hard. I wanted to ask him to explain, but he laughed and said, "Don't let me get on my hobby horse, Mr. Bauer. I am infamous for it."

He made for the driver's door but stopped and turned back. He pointed at the bag.

"Everything is there. On your way back, perhaps we could have a drink in town, and I'll drive you to the airport."

I nodded. "I'd like that."

He drove away, and I carried my two bags back to the

terminal. There I grabbed a cab and told the driver to take me to the port in Georgetown. It was a comparatively short distance, past low, attractive houses set by the river among abundant lush green palms and pine trees. All the way, the driver told me about how the people from Surinam were devious and cunning and could not be trusted. "If they don't stab you comin' in, they gonna stab you goin' out!" he told me, then added that they were basically the same people as in Guyana. "We all brothers an' sisters, right? Indians, the other Indians, Africans, Spanish, Europeans, British. Hey!" He threw his hands in the air, and ash sprayed from his cigarette. "Come on! They should understand that! Right?"

"Right."

As we moved down the broad main street of the small city, past the sugar-brown water of the Demerara River, he asked me, "Where you goin'? You catchin' a boat?"

"St. Homer?"

"I-Takka?" He let out a long, high-pitched hoot. "Maaan, I hope you got sea legs! You got three hours of uuuup and down, up and doooown!" He demonstrated with his hand going up and down over rolling waves, screamed laughter like a parrot, and pounded his steering wheel with the heel of his hand. "I-Takka, maaan. Tha's belong to us, man. You know that? Tha's Guyana. But Surinam, you know, they move in an' took it. You was right to come through Guyana, man. Yeah."

Georgetown is a chaotic, messy city that fails to be delightful because of it. It has beautiful, colonial architecture, colorful markets everywhere you could squeeze in a colorful market, and the people are as open and friendly as people could be, but the town, or as much of it as I saw, was just plain ugly and messy. Everywhere you look, what you see speaks of don't give a damn.

The taxi dropped me outside the ferry terminal on Brickdam Street beside the massive, teaming Stabroek Market. The market stands on the docks at the mouth of the Demerara River, where it spills out into the Atlantic, and the whole area is a nervy, chaotic jumble of fruit, yams, kitsh clothes and jewelry, Black women in blazing robes and headdresses, the rich smells of coffee and spice, and a million shouting voices.

It took me a while, shouldering my way through the crowds, but eventually I found a wooden shack beside the quay. It had a sign over the door which, if you cleaned away the grime, would have read *Ferry Georgetown – I-Takka.* Inside there was a guy leaning his elbows on the counter and his face on his left hand. He looked so bored I found myself checking him for cobwebs.

"I need a passage to I-Takka. When's the next ferry?"

He took a deep breath, blinked his big black eyes, then shifted his gaze from the bright street outside to smile at me.

"Da's gonna be ten thousand five hun'red dollars, my friend. The St. Homer is departin' at eleven a.m. this mornin', sir."

I gave him the money, and he tore a ticket off a pad and handed it to me. Then he leaned forward, frowning, smiling, and shaking his head all at the same time.

"Maaan," he said, "is a *quiet* day. A *quiet* day. I think you gonna be alone on that boat."

The boat turned out to be on the far side of ancient. Probably from the early '60s, it was made of rusty steel that creaked and groaned and clattered when we went over the swollen, rolling waves. The guy had not been far wrong. I was pretty much alone on the boat, aside from a large woman with skin so black it was almost purple and robes and headdress so brilliant and colorful she seemed to vanish inside them. She had an old, battered brown suitcase and sad eyes. I wondered what her story was.

At the far end of the boat, sitting on the rear deck, there was a guy, tall and lanky, with a drinker's nose and grizzled gray hair that still had streaks of blond in it. He had his face plastered against the glass, and he was snoring the snore of the drunk.

It was about a mile and a half to the mouth of the river. As we rounded the sea wall, we sighted the Georgetown Marriott glistening and isolated in the morning sun, and shortly after that, the sea began to swell and the St. Homer started to rear and roll and corkscrew, groaning and creaking as the engine struggled and changed its pitch with every wave. A few miles after that, as the coastline began to fall away behind us, the wind rose and the swell grew higher, with some of the waves spitting salty spray into the air, and now and again, as we slid down the back of a wave, it would explode into great walls of foam on either side of the bow.

That made me go inside and slam the door, and as I gazed out toward the north, I saw brooding black clouds on the horizon. That was not a good omen, I told myself, then dismissed the thought as stupid superstition. I found a seat and lowered myself into it, wondering absently how much the Abrahamic religions and African and native Indian tribal religions had fused and blended here—how much superstition was a part of local culture.

The trip took a little over four and a half hours, and though the threatened storm seemed to dissipate, as we approached the port of Santa Maria, there were still heavy clouds on the northern horizon, and overhead, looking oddly incongruous, a few heavy dark clouds sagged in an otherwise beautiful, clear sky.

The port was a natural cove at the end of a long spit of rock that stretched out into the sea from the main body of the island. At some point, somebody had bothered to cover the place in concrete and build two piers at right angles to each other with a narrow gap left open as an entrance to the harbor. It looked like it might have been a busy place back in the middle of last century, but right now it was all but dead. There were a couple of sailing yachts there, an old schooner, and another ferry similar to the St. Homer. Aside from that, there was little going on.

The port itself was made up of an office that had a sign over the door reading *Port Authority*. The doors and windows were closed and looked like they hadn't been open for a while. There were also a couple of bars and a scattering of houses ranging from very basic dwellings to three-story colonials that were either dilapidated but still elegant or still elegant but dilapidated, depending on whether your glass was half full or half empty.

I grabbed my bags and made my way to the ramp, where I asked one of the sailors where the car rental was. He chewed gum—or something—at me a moment like I must be stupid, then pointed ashore.

"In dah bah," he said. "*Maison La Virgen*."

I didn't bother to thank him. I carried my two Gladstone bags along the quay to the decked terrace of a large, rambling structure. It was set between an empty lot that housed a Mexican palm tree, a Brazilian flame tree, six tires, the remains of a diesel engine and an old brass bed, and a tall, severe, double-fronted colonial building in faded yellow with sage green shutters.

I stepped inside La Virgen. It was dark and empty, but there was a guy with dreadlocks behind the bar polishing glasses. He showed me some very white teeth and asked, "How you doin'?"

"Good. The guy on the boat told me you take care of car rentals."

"He ain't wrong. You want a beer after that crossing?"

"I could use one. Maybe you could tell me how to get to Es Arenal, too. I'm booked in at the I-Takka Hotel."

He wheezed a slow laugh and kept it going till he had a glass full of beer.

"Man," he said as he set it in front of me, "you ain't never gonna get lost on this island. We got just two roads. One goes east-west from here all the way along the island, seven long miles through the Downs to the Pine Valley and up to Le Mole. That's what we call the Main Road. An' then you got a road that that goes south-north from South Faro, the Temple and the lighthouse on the cliff, past Es Arenal, all the way across the Downs to North Faro, which is another lighthouse, an' that is also on a cliff. So man, you follow a road, you come to the crossroads, an' you ain't never gonna be lost."

His laugh was infectious, and I smiled as I took a long pull on the beer. Then he wagged a big finger at me as the laugh faded. "Some people might tell you, dude, just bein' on this island, you already lost!"

As he spoke the words, the tall guy who'd been sleeping on the boat came in. Behind him I could see that a light, warm rain had started to fall. Dreadlocks was saying, "Hey! Klaus, my man! What's it gonna be? You still on beer or you moving up to vodka already?"

Klaus nodded absently at me, leaned on the bar, and reached out a hand.

"Giff me a beer, Dred." Dred was already pouring it. When he handed it over, Klaus took it with a shaking hand and drained the glass. He set it down and sighed. "Make me another," he said and smiled at me. "I am drinking myself to a better world."

"Enjoy the journey," I told him.

Outside, it had grown dark in the time it took me to answer Klaus and turn to Dred. A second after that, the heavens opened, and the pregnant clouds gave birth to a deluge. Dred was wheezing again.

"I can make you a nice grass-fed burger if you ain't in a hurry."

I drained my glass and shook my head. "I'd better make a move or I'll end up headed for a better world with Klaus here. You got the vehicles under cover?"

"Yeah, man. This gonna blow over in ten minutes."

He took me out back where he had half a dozen trucks lined up under a tin roof. The rain made a loud hiss and drummed hard on the corrugated metal. Among the vehicles was a nice black Wrangler, and I pointed to it. "Is it as good as it looks?"

He raised both hands and took a step back. "All my cars, man. All my cars I look after them like they was my babies. There ain't nothin' wrong with any of my cars. You got a problem, you come to Uncle Dred. He gonna fix it for you an' make you a happy man. You wan' a babe, you wan' a joint. All good stuff, dude, happy weed, happy babes. I don't want no problems."

"A happy car will do me for now."

"You got it, dude. That Wrangler's as happy as a truck can get. Beer's on the house. Hope to see you back again."

I paid him, slung my bags in the back, and headed off west along the Main Road: the only road. The rain was heavy, and visibility was low. The car was right-hand drive, and people on the island tended to drive on the left. I say tended because half the time they seemed to drive wherever they hell they wanted to. So I took it slow, remembering what Dred had said, that the rain would blow over in ten minutes or so. Going at twenty miles an hour and sometimes less, it took me almost fifteen minutes to reach the crossroads.

I saw practically nothing of the countryside except for the green and occasionally wooded edges of the road and the deep ditches that were draining away the sudden deluge. I didn't encounter another vehicle, either, going my way or coming head on. The road seemed to be as empty as the island.

Then, suddenly, the crossroads emerged out of the rain. I braked, hydroplaned for twelve feet, and came to a stop with my hood halfway into the intersection. I backed up and saw that Dred had not lied. There was a sign, barely visible, at the side of the road, and it said left was Es Arenal. I indicated out of habit—nobody was going to see it—and turned left.

The rain didn't stop, but it began to ease as a strong wind picked up out of the south. On my right I began to see a rocky landscape that ascended toward what looked like a dense pine forest in the distance. On my left there was a deep ditch which I could now see fed canals that intersected the waterlogged fields of corn, watermelons, and fruit trees.

And then I saw something that should not have been there. At first it looked like a bundle of sodden rags being flapped around by the wind. But as I slowed and looked harder, I saw that the bundle of rags had hair, and that too was being blown this way and that by the wind. I stopped and put my hazard lights on.

I swung down from the cab and was instantly drenched by the downpour. I grabbed a luminous triangle from the trunk and, wiping the rain from my eyes, stuck it in the road twenty feet behind the Jeep. Then I ran and scrambled down into the ditch, knee deep in sludge and water. I waded across and had real trouble getting out the other side, slipping and scrambling in the loose mud. I had to crawl out and struggle to my feet, covered in sludge. From there I ran, ankle deep in the water-logged field, to where the large bundle lay motionless, but for the cloth and hair, whipped this way and that.

I got down on my knees beside it and started to remove the rags, wiping the water from my face as it fell. But I already knew what I was going to find. She must have been fourteen or fifteen when she was alive. She'd been pretty. She would probably have grown into a beautiful woman. She was blond and very pale of skin. Her eyes, which now stared unblinking into a gray, bellying sky, were blue.

She had contusions to her neck and face. She had been gripped hard, but she had not been strangled. There was no swelling, her tongue was not protruding, nor were her eyes bulging.

I trudged back to the ditch, brushing the rain from my eyes with my fingers. I struggled across and back up to the road and collected the luminous reflective triangle I'd placed behind the Jeep. With it in my hand, I made my way back to the body and placed it by her head so I'd be able to tell the sheriff exactly where I found her. Then, with extreme difficulty, I picked her up and slung her over my shoulder. Rigor had not set in, and she was small, but even so, a dead body is difficult to move, and the extra ninety to a hundred pounds made me sink deeper into the sodden mire and made walking a real struggle. Getting her into the ditch was difficult, getting her out of it was impossible, and in the end, I had to use the winch on the front of the truck to drag her up.

Dignity belongs to the living. There is no dignity in death, whoever you are.

By the time I'd laid her on the back seat, I was a mess, saturated and covered from head to toe in mud, and I was exhausted. I stood for a moment letting the rain rinse me off. Then I got behind the wheel and set off again for Es Arenal, the capital of the island. I had a bad feeling. I was going to have to deliver this child to the sheriff. And any sheriff worth his salt was going to put me right at the top of his list of suspects. I could not afford to get arrested, much less be investigated or go on trial. But then, as the brigadier had asked, where do you draw that pragmatic line? Neither could I let this child lie dead, neglected in a field, and drive on by, not if I was going to remain human.

The gods would have to decide. The brigadier would have said that was irony.

# CHAPTER 3

IT WAS ABOUT A MILE AND A HALF, AND AS THE RAIN began to ease, lights began to flicker in the distance, ahead and to my right. Then I began to see, through the misty haze of the rain, a small town maybe half a mile up ahead. The road fed straight into a central plaza that was paved in red and white. At the center there was a garden with jacaranda trees, rose bushes, and benches set around a fountain. Beside it was a statue of a guy in a tricorn hat.

The rain now stopped as suddenly as it had started. Overhead, the clouds were breaking up, and the blacktop had become steel blue with reflected light. I slowed and counted six cars around the square. The newest one was a thirty-year-old convertible Rover 216 Cabrio. The oldest was a red 1960s Buick, complete with wings. Straight ahead of me was a large, three-story colonial building with a Georgian portico over an expanding flight of seven shallow steps. The windows had green, wooden shutters, all of which were closed. It had the air of a city hall. To the left of that was a terrace of houses in varying states of disrepair.

To the right there was a butchers, and next to him was a baker. Maybe the next was a candlestick maker, but I couldn't see because at a right angle to it, obscuring the road, was another building. This building was illuminated, and light flooded out onto the sidewalk and the blacktop. It was a bar. It had a blue neon sign outside that said *The Sea Breeze* in flowing letters and a picture of a fish under the word breeze, swimming in the opposite direction. Water had obviously gotten into the wiring somewhere because the sign was flickering on and off.

There were no cars moving, so I turned the wrong way into the square and came to a stop outside the bar. I pulled the dead girl from the back seat, cradled her in my arms, and carried her to the entrance. I worked the handle with my foot, pushed the door open, and stepped inside.

It wasn't even half full, but there were more people there than I'd seen so far on the whole island. There was a guy behind the bar. He was white and blond, but he had dreadlocks to his waist that looked like they might have colonies of rodents and insects living in them. The reggaeton was throbbing in the background. The guy behind the bar stopped what he was doing because apparently he couldn't put a glass on the bar and gape at the same time.

The glass of beer was intended for one of four guys standing opposite him on this side of the bar. They were all dressed in jeans and had identical khaki shirts with epaulettes. There were three cream cowboy hats on the counter. The fourth was on its owner's head. Those four guys were staring but not gaping. Around the room there were four tables. Two were occupied by families, the other two by couples.

The guys at the bar watched me, but nobody moved or said anything. I ignored them and made my way to one of the unoccupied tables. I hooked my foot around the leg and dragged it over to the next table, kicked the chairs out of the way, and laid the limp body down. Her cold, bare feet stuck out at the end. Her jeans were caked with mud, like her blouse and her hair.

I turned and studied at the four guys at the bar. I saw that the one with the hat had a star pinned to his shirt.

"Are you gentlemen deputies? Is one of you the sheriff?" I pointed at the body. "She's not sleeping. She's dead."

The guy with the star answered. "I am the sheriff on this island. Sheriff Jeremiah Scott. These are my deputies. Who are you, and what in the name of hell have you got there?"

"I'm Harry Bauer, and this is a dead girl. I spotted her body in a field, a mile and a half up the road. She was lying face down in the mud. I have left a reflective triangle to mark the spot."

They just stared at me. I'd never seen anything like it. Outside I heard distant thunder. The barman, still holding the glass of beer, the three deputies and the sheriff, and the families and couples sitting at their tables. They all just stared.

I shifted my gaze to the gaping barman. I spoke quietly. "Can we have that fucking music off out of respect for this dead child?"

He put down the glass, closed his mouth, and hurried to turn off the reggaeton. Silence settled on the room.

"You want to take it easy there, son." It was the sheriff. "There's no call to be cursing."

"There isn't? Does anybody know who this girl is?" Nobody said anything. I said to the sheriff, "Does anybody give a damn? Are you going to look at the body? Are you going to call a doctor to certify her death, and cause of death?"

He raised an eyebrow at me. "Yeah, I'm gonna look at the body, Mr. Bauer, but I reckon you need to cool down a few degrees." He turned to one of his deputies, who was clean shaven and looking very alarmed. "Rishi, go get Doctor Brown.

Tell her..." His eyes shifted to me. "Tell her the Middleton girl has been found by a stranger. She's dead."

Rishi made for the door but stopped dead and looked back at the sheriff when I said, "Are you just going to take my word for that, or are you going to check for yourself?"

He blinked slowly. "I can see from here she's dead, Mr. Bauer. And before you start making crazy insinuations, I should remind you that right now it seems you was the last person to see her alive."

I shook my head. I reached in my jacket pocket, pulled out my ferry ticket, and stepped over to him. I held out the ticket. "I was the first person to see her dead, Sheriff. Somebody else was the last to see her alive. That ticket, and the testimony of Dred at the *Maison La Virgen*, where I rented my Jeep, should make it clear I was either at sea or at the port when this girl was murdered."

I pushed past him and between the two deputies to lean on the bar and tell the bartender, who was gaping again, "Get me a beer and a hamburger."

I heard the door slam and figured Deputy Rishi had gone to get the doctor.

"It's on me." I turned and looked. The sheriff handed me back the ticket and gave the barman the nod. He said again, "It's on me, Ned." To me he said, "Gratitude for what you done, Mr. Bauer. Most people would have driven right on by. We don't mean to be discourteous, but we don't see many outsiders on I-Takka." I noticed he pronounced it as though the T was a Th. "So we tend to be a bit suspicious. No harm done."

I raised the glass Ned had brought me. "No harm, no foul. Cheers."

"Cheers." We both drank, and as he set down his glass, he

said, "So what brings you to this remote corner of the globe, Mr. Bauer?"

I set down my own glass and arched an eyebrow at him. "That accent's not from I-Takka, Sheriff. It's not Caribbean or South American. I'd place it somewhere in the southwest of the United States. Arizona?"

He smiled and came to lean on the bar beside me. "Winslow. You can believe it or not, but I was born on the corner of Kinsley Avenue and Route 66. And you're asking me what brings an Arizona cowboy to St. Homer to become sheriff in a place that would normally have a constable."

I gave my head a little twitch that said he wasn't wrong.

"Well, it's a long story, Mr. Bauer, and maybe one day I'll tell it to you over a couple of beers, but right now it looks as though I might be investigating Maisy Middleton's homicide, so I am going to ask you again real polite, what brings you to our island?"

Thunder rolled again in the distance. At the same time, bright sunshine leaned through the window and framed black shadows across the floor.

"Curiosity," I said. "I like traveling in places off the beaten track. I was reading about Surinam and Guyana, and I-Takka came up. I thought I'd come and have a look."

"Ever been to Alaska? That's pretty remote and off the beaten track."

I sighed. "Subtlety ain't the big thing here, huh, Sheriff? Alaska is also a preferred destination for serial killers. I know that, Sheriff. I am not a serial killer, and if I were, you have two or three difficult questions to answer."

"Yeah? To me it looks like it would answer all of 'em."

"First, why the hell would I bring her here instead of leaving her where I killed her? Second, have you ever come across a serial killer whose MO included taking the body of his victim to her home or her village? Third, why the hell would I kill her in the middle of a field during a rainstorm instead of doing the job in my truck and dropping her in the sea at one of the Faros? Fourth, and maybe most important, what the hell was she doing out there, alone, in the middle of that storm? What are you suggesting, Sheriff? That I arrived on the ferry, collected my car at *Maison La Virgen,* drove here through the storm and, along the way, with visibility down to twenty or thirty yards, found this girl walking alone, in the downpour, in a light dress, picked her up, and killed her? Then what did I do, dump her in a muddy field before collecting her again and bringing her here? Then I refer you to my first three questions. And the fourth, come to that."

He grunted. "You a cop? You talk like a cop."

"No. I was a soldier. I've seen a lot of death in places off the beaten track."

"Special ops?"

I nodded once. "Where do the Middletons live?"

He jerked his head to his right, the opposite direction from the field where I had found Maisy. "Down along Beachfront Road a ways."

"How far a ways?"

"Half a mile maybe. Don't go thinking about taking them the news, Mr. Bauer. I have a job to do here, and I don't want you interfering, y'hear? You booked into a hotel?"

"The I-Takka."

"That's opposite here, on the other side of the square. I suggest you check in, get yourself a shower and some rest, and let me and the doc do our jobs."

"Do I get to eat the burger you so generously invited me to?"

He didn't get to answer that because the door opened and Rishi came in with the doc, followed by a gust of cool, rain-washed breeze.

The doc was wearing dirty jeans, a stained military shirt, and muddy walking boots. Her afro hair was tied back with a thick, black elastic band. Her skin was dark, but her features were more native Caribbean than African. She had a big, brown leather satchel in her hand which for some reason looked oddly incongruous with the jeans, the military shirt, and the afro hair.

She approached the table and stood motionless, looking down at the dead girl for a long moment. Then she stroked her cheek with the back of her fingers. She felt for a pulse in her wrist and her neck and after a moment pulled her cell from her pocket and held it to her own mouth.

"Maisy Middleton, pronounced dead at the Sea Breeze at fifteen minutes after five p.m." And she gave the date. She put her cell away and bent to examine the girl's face and throat, then her hands and fingers. "Who found her?"

"I did. She was about a mile and a half up the road, face down in the field, on the right as you're leaving the village."

She glanced at me, then down at my hands.

"May I see...?"

She trailed off because I had stepped forward, unbuttoning my sleeves and rolling them up. I held out both hands, palms down. She studied them, then my forearms, and looked over at the sheriff. He approached, frowning. She told him, "I need to do a proper examination, but you can see here, her jaw? There is a very clear imprint of what appears to be a very large right-hand fist. However strong the man is, his fist will be bruised by the bone. Also, you see the bruising to her throat? Look at her fingernails." She lifted the hand and indicated the fingertips and the nails. There was skin, flesh, and blood under them. "Whoever did this has a bruised fist and badly scratched hands and/or forearms."

The sheriff nodded a few times. "Seems to put you in the clear, Mr. Bauer."

"I told you, Sheriff. I found her. Your time of death is going to be almost impossible. It'll be some time between when I found her and when she was last seen, which will probably put me on the ferry from Georgetown." I glanced at him. "But it might also tell you what the hell a girl of her age was doing out alone, more than a mile from home, in the middle of a field in a rain storm."

"You leave that to me, Mr. Bauer. You've been more than helpful enough already."

I turned to the doctor. "Doctor Brown, if you need me, I'll be at the I-Takka Hotel, across the square."

She nodded once, examining my face with eyes that were not hostile but were definitely not friendly either. She said, "Thank you," then turned to the sheriff. "Can you have your boys load her in the back of my truck and bring her into the mortuary?" She handed over the keys and added, "I'll see you there."

She stepped outside with me. Overhead, the sky was turning to evening. I pulled open the driver's door of the Wrangler. She paused on the sidewalk and pointed to the big building I had seen on my arrival that looked to me like a city hall.

"Drive me to the town hall? It's on your way."

"Sure, get in."

She climbed in, and we slammed the doors. As I pulled away, she said, "Are you some kind of cop?"

"Straight to the point, huh? What would some kind of cop

be?" I turned to look at her. "And more to the point, whose jurisdiction would he have?"

"Are you dodging the question to avoid answering it? If so, you just answered it."

"No, I am not a cop. Why do you ask?"

She smiled. "Twice. You dodged the question twice. You're not a cop, but I asked you if you were some kind of cop."

I had pulled up outside City Hall—their town hall. It was all closed up and dark, but there was a side alley, and down there I could see the rear lights of her truck, where Maisy's body was being delivered. She opened the door and swung down. Before slamming the door, she said, "I might need you to come round tomorrow when I do the autopsy. I want you to explain some things to me."

"You want me to come in now?"

She shook her head. "Not now, tomorrow."

I nodded. "Sure."

She slammed the door, and I covered the short distance to the hotel.

Scan the QR code below to purchase
JUSTICE WITHOUT MERCY.

Or go to: righthouse.com/justice-without-mercy

www.ingramcontent.com/pod-product-compliance
Lightning Source LLC
Chambersburg PA
CBHW031958190626
46808CB00018B/1901